Edward Harry William Meyerstein (1889-1952) was born in Hampstead, London. A man of letters, he worked for a period in the manuscript room of the British Museum. He wrote numerous books including the collection of poems *Symphonies* (1915), *A Life of Thomas Chatterton* (1930), and the novel *Séraphine* (1936).

I0602954

SNUGGLY BOOKS

E. H. W. MEYERSTEIN

BOLLOND

THIS IS A SNUGGLY BOOK

ISBN: 978-1-64525-171-2

BOLLOND

I

Pevensey is intolerably dull at this time of year, better than London, where somebody is always asking you questions, but dull all the same. Since I came last night, I have looked out constantly on the flats and the martello towers; I sat up in bed half the night in this pursuit, and only fell asleep with the dawn. It is strange, as there is nothing appealing about them. This morning after breakfast my eyes were at the same game, so I made up my mind to write something so as to rest them, until Dorothy comes on Thursday. What to write? My life up to the present time, a queer affair. Why not? I have lived in a more or less literary set for the last five months, and stumbled across a lot of books that I was quite unable to understand. I ought to have the trick of the pen; no harm in trying; perhaps I may make the future clear to me. So long as my eyes stop staring at the distance!

II

I suppose I must start off with my birth. That makes me think that my life is almost at an end. Why should a fellow of my age write his life? To ease his mind? Absurd! Much better go for a swim in the sea. To earn a little money? That's more sensible, but there are sounder ways than pandering to the craze for novels of modern life. Really I haven't a leg to stand on, except that there is absolutely nothing else for me to do in this God-forsaken place.

III

Seventeen and a half years ago I was born in a country house in Leicestershire, pleasant enough spot for a gentleman's son. My mother was an invalid as long as I can remember. Invalids do not feel like other people; not that Mother was not fond of me, but she could not take a proper interest in me. She could only say, "Be a good boy. Kiss me", and stroke my hair. Sometimes she read to me, but in so monotonous a voice that it was clear she did not take in the sense of the book. So naturally I did not listen. She had beautiful brown hair and grey eyes like Dorothy; illness made them shine. I never looked on her as a real person, real persons get angry and show preferences; everything was the same to Mother lying on the sofa in the drawing-room.

My father was a sportsman with a bad temper, extremely fond of his wife. They would sit together for hours in the evening without a word. Almost the first thing I remember is Father bringing me a picture-book, and opening it at a large coloured plate of a tiger. "There, Reggie," he said, "you'll go out and shoot them one day, won't you?" I believe I turned over the page, for he flushed and, turning to my mother, growled, "The boy's got nothing of me about him."

As I grew up, Father became a sort of irritable institution that kept me going. He taught me to ride, which I hated, and made several lame attempts to get me interested in cricket and football. He put me down for his old school: I won't disgrace it by mentioning its name.

IV

To my nurse I owe most of my nature. She was a reclaimed vagabond, whom my mother saved from going back to the streets by finding her a husband in our under-gardener. No doubt entirely without meaning to do so, she gave me the fruit of her old experience. That is why now I take far greater pleasure in the jokes of street-cads and loafers than in the probably much more amusing humours of the class from which I spring. Molly instilled vanity and idleness into me, I know. "Isn't it a pretty moppet?" she would say; "Hold up your head and be proud of your beauty," and once, which I cannot forget, when I dropped a cup, "He can't do wrong, why? Because he's a pretty boy." Molly, I am in need of you; you could raise my spirits now. I wish after we lost our money I had kept up with you and found out where you meant to live. Many a time have I longed for your advice; I should have done what you told me. Unfortunately I cannot recall a single fact or story—they were never fairy stories—that she repeated, more, I admit, to herself than me (as if it pleased her to think about her past with a little child playing around, who might or might not overhear), except a general impression that life, for such as she was once, did not offer any problems of conduct. There was no "Shall I say this or that?" or "Shall I be thought a liar if I say this?", no "must" or "must not", you did things and took the consequences. There was joy and sorrow, pleasure and trouble, but no degradation, or sinking into a lower state because you were found out. Drunkenness, robbery, and even murder were familiar to her, but the households to which these un-pleasantnesses attached themselves did not lose caste.

Naturally I preferred her to my parents.

V

My second brother being twelve years my senior, it follows that my brothers have not entered into my life at all, just as if they were a remote branch of the family. They were seldom at home; on these rare occasions they would make me a present, and always put an enquiry about me at the end of their letters. They were both on active service when my mother died. And later, when my father was carried off by a stroke in London, though they heard of the crash and the sale of our house, they could do nothing more than offer to pay for the remainder of my schooling. But by that time I had left under circumstances that must be told, not long before my father's death. Since then they have communicated only with my aunt, his sister, who stepped into the breach and has treated me since Christmas, rightly or wrongly, as a paid outcast. I have written to neither of my brothers through motives of delicacy, strange though it may seem.

VI

My early education was directed, not towards my good but my entry into a big public school, consequently I retained nothing of real value. My father's heart was set on giving me the appearance of an English country gentleman, and no doubt he reflected that, though he had failed in making a sportsman of me, I could swagger with the best of them. A tutor was found, Mr. Hincham, at some expense, I believe, who had the reputation of forcing the most uncompromising dunces through entrance examinations. I hardly care to recall what I suffered at his hands. He had liberty to punish me to his liking; this generally took the following form. I had to stand at attention in the middle of the room for half an hour; every time I moved, he told me to stand easy, while he waggled a cane between my legs—extremely painful. His first words to me were, "What did Miss Floscombe teach you?" (She was my mother's companion who acted as governess.) I said, "Why don't you ask her?"

"Clearly no manners," he said. After that he never missed the chance of a fling at her incapacity, not of course in her presence, which hurt me. He was a tall man with the air of a soldier, and impressed me with the truth, which I have never had reason to doubt, that it does not matter if one is a fool, provided one is smart, straight-backed, and ready with replies. He gave me lists of Greek and Latin writers to repeat, telling me very little about them, so that I should not look ignorant if any were mentioned. At my viva voce I was asked who Seneca was, and said, "Latin philosopher, who bled himself to death," pleasing the examiner. Mr. Hincham never gratified my curiosity if a subject interested me and I wanted to know more about it, and thus succeeded in fixing what he had taught me more definitely in my mind than if he had mingled profit with pleasure....

So in two and a half years I was a complete sham, a boy without one decent interest, save bird's-nesting, which I shared with one or two village lads whose fathers were poachers, thoroughly convinced of his stupidity and duty to conceal it from others, well-groomed and tidy, upright and obedient, a regular little man of the world. I passed into the Lower Shell, classical side.

VII

I was to spend five years at school, involving, had I completed them, a waste of about £1,000. My father would then have done his part, and I would be left to find my groove. But well after I was sixteen a couple of misfortunes befell our family that are largely responsible for my present haphazard way of living. I may say at once that I have no notion of business, and cannot explain how, having money, my father came to lose it. He did not speculate, I know, and, though his temper was of the worst, in serious predicaments he kept it and blamed no one. The news was broken to me, at school, by Molly, and I can almost remember the words of her letter: "Read this when nobody is by. The old home is to be sold. It has been sad enough since the mistress died. The master is going to do work for the government in London, Hal says. You are not to be told anything yet awhile; but, my dear, I thought it well to say that if you have a friend to stay with these holidays, stay with him and don't come home."

Now I was in the school corps; everyone was then. I took care to play an instrument in the band, so as to get off as many drills as possible. It happened that one or two of the boldest spirits were buglers, older than I, who more than once had asked me to drink with them in camp, when it was easy to smuggle in beer. Lately they had actually contracted with a publican to let them have some whisky on field day. The inn was a little way out of the town, and their plan was, when we marched past on our way to the station, one of us would slip out of line, get the bottle, put it into his haversack, and join up again. There was practically no supervision in the band, prefects scorned it as beneath their dignity, and the band master was a blear-eyed old fossil who liked a drop himself. I was deputed to call for the bottle, and the plan would have undoubtedly succeeded had not one of the junior masters, returning from his mother's funeral, strolled up Station Road unseen by me, just as I dropped into the door. My friends could not warn me to stay where I was, so I walked out right into his arms, without an excuse, which would in any case have been difficult to find. It was a turn no one could have expected, as that station was hardly ever used by people connected with the school, and the chance of a master returning at 8.45 a.m. on a field day was one in a thousand. As it was, he told me to stay there while he had a word with the bandmaster; then the procession moved on, and he and I trudged slowly back to the empty school-buildings. It occurs to me now that, had I pleaded with him and showed contrition, before the haversack was examined, I might have escaped more lightly, though I had already been flogged once, last term, for idleness; but I maintained a stubborn silence until we reached our house, when I asked him what he meant to do about me. He looked me straight in the face and said, "Nothing, except report to your housemaster that I saw you enter a public house." Then he walked back to his rooms. There was I in uniform with the whisky; how get rid of it? More from nervousness than any other reason I lugged the haver sack round, when who should step out but my house master. "What does this mean, Bollond?" he asked. "Oh," I said, "I am feeling ill, and the Sergeant said I had better come back and report myself to you, Sir." As I moved towards the house, he called out after me, "What have you got in your haversack? Take it off and hand it over." (The bottle bulged of course.) So it came out. In a few minutes I was standing before the headmaster in his study. I refused to mention names. Sentence of immediate expulsion was passed. I went back to my house, changed into an ordinary suit, packed things for the night in a hand-bag, and left by a train from the other station in less than two hours, playbox and trunk being sent after me. My housemaster's farewell speech was, "Never let me see you near my front door again. Good luck to you." Only two days before had I received Molly's letter.

VIII

"Now you've done it!" I said aloud on the platform, so that a lady turned to have a look at me. Just turned seventeen and disgraced, how should I approach my father? Mother, thank Heaven, had died not quite a year ago. In any case I should have to wait a couple of hours in London for the next train home, which would land me there at night; we were almost four miles from a small station. Go to town and see what happens. With a mind absolutely blank I walked across London from one station to the other, and left my hand bag in the cloakroom at St. Pancras. It was one forty-five or thereabouts. I lunched at the buffet, and, mounting a bus, got down at Marble Arch and walked through the Park. Seeing no hope in myself, I eyed the passers-by inquisitively, until one girl, returning my glance, dropping her reticule. Picking it up, I returned it to her with a pleading expression (I knew how to plead now.) "Thank you," she said impassively; "are you walking this way?" So we fell into conversation.

"Don't think me rude, but why are you not at school?"

"Because I have just left."

"Rather sudden?"

"These things happen."

"Sacked? You don't seem to mind."

"Don't I?"

"Are you going home, boy?"

"I hardly know as yet."

"How much cash have you, or shouldn't I ask? Shall we turn here?"

"By all means." (We turned.) "Two pounds odd. They paid my fare. Rather decent of them, don't you think?"

"They could hardly do less; but I don't see any reason for sacking you." I told her the reason; she agreed that I was unlucky. I must certainly not do anything rash. Why not have tea with her? She lived in Jermyn Street. There was time to walk, unless I had an objection. I was under no misapprehension as to her way of life, though I had not spoken to one of her class before. She was so amiable and sympathetic that to go with her seemed the most natural thing in the world.

"You are a nice boy," she said musingly, "and you must not be spoilt. You don't know how many young lives I have seen spoilt."

"Tell me about them," I cried; "I do so much want to get away from myself."

"You wouldn't be interested, Harry. I shall call you Harry," she said.

"My name is Roy." Why did I lie, I wonder?

"Well, Roy," she went on, watching me suspiciously, unless I mistook, "you will find when you are my age—don't ask it—that the ugly people are after all the nicest, and that most of the pretty ones, male and female, come to grief, somehow or other."

"What is your name?" I asked, not particularly anxious to hear her philosophy.

"Georgette, I will give you a card when you go."

We talked theatres mainly on the walk, as if we were dancing partners, but she imparted a sense of freedom and blamelessness, most grateful to one who had pretty well decided that he could not look anyone in the face after the morning's event.

Her room two floors above a shop, was the cleanest imaginable, with fashion plates pinned on the white walls and a short stick in the corner nearest the washstand. Before I left she had given me, besides many kisses, the following advice, which she wrote on the back of an envelope with her name and address:

1. To go home that night without fail.
2. To see Molly first and tell her everything.
3. To be guided entirely by Molly's advice.
4. Not to quarrel with my father or answer him back, whatever he said.
5. To write to her, Georgette, even for money, if I needed it.

I don't know how I came to tell her about Molly, but she said in the course of the afternoon that I would tell her everything, implying that she knew me better than my own mother, of whom I took care to drop no word; on that point I was firmness itself.

IX

By the time I had reclaimed my bag at St. Pancras and eaten some sandwiches I was fairly joyless again; so I approached the bookstall to find something to read on the journey. A purple-covered novel was conspicuous. It started with a father beating his son for sitting in a public house, and I wondered if I should be beaten when I got home. The hero struck me as rather dogged and obstinate, not brave, stupid also and with far too good opinion of himself. The book depressed me, and, having sucked it fairly dry, I left it on the bookstall and bought a paper. It was a raw October night with a full moon. The old ticket collector recognized me. "Home early this time, Mr. Reginald." That cut me. I was the only passenger to that station, and it seemed, the one human creature abroad at the hour. The lanes were empty of lovers, and the trees as still as goal-posts. Lights were out in the lodge, so I knocked three or four times at the bedroom window. I heard Molly call out sleepily, "Hal, what's that?" Then Hal raised himself and roared, "Who the devil are you?" while Molly lit a candle. Before I could speak, she caught sight of me through the curtains, and cried, "Oh, Master Reggie!", and ran to open the door. For some reason I could not move from the window. Hal opened it, and I dropped my head between his hands, more tired than sobbing. In a moment Molly was round and drew me into the lodge, refusing to hear my tale till I had drunk something warm. Hal produced—oh horror!—whisky. "Take it away," I shouted; "it is the cause of all the mischief and my ruin"; and putting an arm round Molly's neck, so strong and comforting, I blurted out my miserable enterprise and its result.

Their faces were serious, but Hal, scratching his head, offered his opinion, "It seems to me, Master Reggie, that this is about as good a thing as can have happened to you, for who knows, if the dangers of drink had not been brought home to you now, you might have learned them when it was too late. There is always a mistake we could have avoided, and one we couldn't have avoided, and no power on earth could prevent that teacher from nabbing you; but you know what the bottle stands for and where it brings a man."

"Be quiet and don't lecture him," said Molly; "he's a pretty boy and can't do wrong, no, that he can't, even if the master sends him off tomorrow without a penny in his pocket."

On the strength of this remark I drank off the whisky pulling a wry face.

"He's no drunkard!" exclaimed Hal, clapping me on the back so that I choked. We agreed that attempting to keep anything back from my father would be a fatal policy; the debatable point was whether I should go to the house then and there—it was close on one, or wait until breakfast: I of course burned to have the ordeal over. "There is never any harm in a sleep," said Hal. "Yes," said I, "if you *can* sleep."

A shake-down was made for me—Molly, I know, would have turned out of bed to make room—and I slept soundly without dreaming, in my clothes, but without my shoes, which Hal insisted on cleaning, until eight o'clock, long after the others had risen. "Drink this off," commanded Molly, "and go at once. You can wash after you've seen the master." The tea made my stomach sink even lower, if that were possible; and after tying my shoes with such vigour, to cover my panic, that a lace broke, I put on my hat and coat, took my bag, and slunk up the drive.

The door was open, so I did not have to face Bullivant, the butler, but walked, as I was, hat in hand, into the dining-room. My father was eating mushrooms; the morning's post lay open at his side. "I have come back, sir," I said at once with a fine rush of words, "because I am expelled for buying whisky for some members of the corps, whose names I refused to betray."

"I know all about that," said my father. "Where did you sleep last night?"

"At the lodge. I came by the last train, and didn't want to rouse the house."

"Have you had any breakfast?"

"Only a cup of tea."

"Sit down and listen to me. Yes, take off your things and hang them outside."

When I came back, a place was laid for me. Second escape from Bullivant. I fell to with relish; no use to pretend that I was off my feed. My father said nothing till I was at the marmalade stage; then he crystallized not only his whole knowledge of me, but his plans for any future and the story of his own misfortune into hardly more than a dozen sentences.

"From a worldly point of view you have ruined yourself, but that is no reason why you should not make money, sometime or other. I will tell you your exact position: when you are of age, you are entitled to a small annuity under your mother's will, barely enough to live on in these times. I am penniless. If I died tomorrow, you would not be any better off. When this place is sold, and sold it must be, I doubt if I shall have enough to pay my creditors. Next week I take up work in the Censor's Office to enable me to live. I cannot support you till you are of age. The war is not over yet. Your obvious course is to go to London and enlist as a private in a regiment of your choice, and, if possible, work your way up the ranks; I see no other immediate future for you. Here are five pounds. Don't let me hear from you again until you are in khaki. Go as soon as you like; I won't detain you."

I left the house at once, third and last escape from Bullivant.

X

Perhaps my father's words had inspired me with some of his pride, for I marched away from the house triumphant, with head in air, purposely ignoring the lodge, where Molly no doubt was observing me from a window, and gained the station in record time, well under an hour, only waiting twenty minutes for a train. Before we had passed two stations, I regretted my haste, for, diving into my pocket for any odd change, I clutched Georgette's envelope. Remembering a saying of my tutor, "It is always too late to repent," I brushed the thought aside and concentrated on my plan of action. Had I the slightest desire to be a soldier? No. The war, I was convinced, could not go on much longer; a year would see the end of it. As things were, my age exempted me; the Army therefore had no claim, and my father was simply driving me into making a false declaration in order to absolve himself of responsibility. The alternative, when my money was spent, was starvation in London. I could not starve, the idea was inconceivable, but at first I would consult appearances.

I went to the Kingsley Hotel and booked a room for three days. Sitting down in one of the public rooms, I wrote three letters; I believed in the number three that day. The first was to my father to say that I was a private in the 3rd Battalion of the Northumberland Fusiliers, C Coy., hurriedly scrawled and, blotted, and dated the day following, when I posted it at Knightsbridge.

The second, to Molly, ran somewhat in this manner:

"Dearest old Nurse, I couldn't face you this morning, really I could not, turned away from the old home that I shall never see again. I am a soldier, Molly, think of that, and perhaps I shall be killed. I can give you no address but this, where an old friend of mine is staying, whom I met just now in the street. I want you to pack up some old clothes of mine, collars, ties and socks too, if you can, and send them him, or rather to me here—for I shall be in London, drilling, for some little time,

I expect. He wants clothes badly, as he is very poor. So if you can do as I ask you, *of course without letting my father know*, I shall be eternally grateful. Please thank Hal for his good advice—this is a temperance hotel.

"Yours affectionately,
"R. Bolland."

I wrote on the envelope in a plain round hand, unlike my own, for fear my father might have all letters brought to him, in case I tried to borrow of the servants, for he might or might not believe what I had told him. The third was to Georgette, saying that I was turned out of home and in London with nothing to do, when would she see me: reply by return. The two last I posted at once, and lunched off macaroni in Soho.

XI

Eating, I thought of money and nothing else; with the utmost economy my total would only last a week. As the rest of the day was a complete blank and at my disposal, I determined to find where the cheapest lodgings were to be had, barring the East End. Mind you, I hardly knew London at all, yet it seemed friendly. There must have been a reason for that, though I haven't the wits to pitch on it. I strolled through Bloomsbury until I came to Marchmont Street. A middle-aged chap with a wooden leg was lolling against the railings of number three. I promptly bearded him.

"You've come to the right shop, mister," he said. "I wouldn't say this to everybody, but I like the look of you. Play the poor mouth and always be on your beam ends, and you'll be able to live here quite comfortably. My name's Schmuck."

He was so amiable that I thought he wanted to swindle me.

"Roy Bollond's my name," I said in a manly tone, "and I don't care who knows it. I'm staying at the Kingsley Hotel at present with my father, who has work at the Censor's Office, but we've quarrelled and he has turned me out with five shillings a week" ('Are you *quite* mad?' said a voice in my head, but I went on, disregarding); "at present I have fifteen shillings."

"You mean to earn a living?" he said.

"If I can. I'm no trouble in a house; I'll run errands," and my voice broke quite naturally.

The man turned his head away: "Come here this time tomorrow, and I'll see what I can do for you."

"Do you really mean it?" I asked. He gave me his hand.

As soon as I had turned the corner, I asked the way to the nearest stationer's. There I bought a notebook with pencil and elastic band, and made a note of my new address, in case I should forget it. Woodenleg was a friend, or I couldn't see straight.

XII

I had tea (a couple of buns) near Southampton Row, and returned to the hotel, where I sat for the rest of the evening, listening to country cousins discussing their first experiences of town, and reading the daily papers, especially the advertisement columns. I allowed myself eighteenpence for the theatre, but meant to postpone that pleasure as long as possible. I dined in for the first and last time. I was not particular about food, and there were cheaper places in Soho. I was sitting half asleep In the best arm-chair in the smoking-room which I secured by being first to leave the table-d'hôte room, when it occurred to me that I might improve the occasion by writing to the fellows, partly on whose account I had suffered expulsion.

"Dear F. J. (I wrote), I hope you and L. enjoyed the field day, minus the latest addition to Sticky's cellar. Of course you know all about my luck, rotten I call it, but there it is. I am in London, supposed to be in the Army, for the governor wants me there really kicking my heels. I have thought of the stage, and am going tomorrow to have a talk with a girl I know, who may get me on. Send me news of yourselves. Am I the only victim? I hope so. This address will find me, though I am only here a day or two more.

"R. B."

I am able to give this word for word, as I rescued it only the other day from the pocket of an old suit; it made me laugh so much. It was not sent because I reflected that my friends might be under suspicion, and it would be quite in Sticky's way to open all the letters that came for them during the next fort-night.

XIII

The next day brought a note from Georgette, asking me to lunch in her room at one. She had a game pie. I spent the morning in the British Museum, which had been a good friend to me. It is the wannest place in London on cold days, and the coolest on hot ones. Lately I have obtained a reader's ticket, but that is off the point. "Hallo, old fellow!" cried Georgette, who was painted up to the eyes. (The pie was there right enough, and a good one it proved.) "Years since we met! Are you stony?"

"Not altogether," I said, "but out of work. The governor says I must go for a soldier, but I am under age."

"Did you tell him so?"

"No, I was too flabbergasted; I walked out of the house."

"You haven't broken with your father?" (in a timorous tone).

I laughed. "Not exactly; but he doesn't expect to hear from me till I am in uniform, so I am in uniform." The joke did not strike her as funny. She shaded her eyes with one hand.

"A friend of mine, who sent me this pie, has an invalid relative, who wants a young person to stay with her—she has a maid. I don't know whether she could afford to pay very much, but board and lodging would be free, of course."

"Aunt in Brighton, I suppose. Who is this friend of yours?"

"Don't be inquisitive."

It was perfectly clear that she had me framed in her mind as a young ne'er-do-well without money; in spite of the meal her greeting was harder than two days ago. I eyed her candidly.

"What do you think I am fit for—an actor?"

She went over to the bed and took half a crown from her reticule; handing it me, she said, "Now come over here and be kissed."

I left the house half an hour later, feeling quite a different person, though what kind of person it would be almost impossible to explain, and walked to Marchmont Street. My wooden-legged friend was standing outside number three.

"What's your news?" he asked.

"Only that I've made half a crown," I said.

"Come inside," said he, "and don't say anything until I tell you. It all depends on whether Miss Lucy thinks you are honest."

We went in together. "I'll see him here," said a sharp girlish voice, so we got no farther than the passage.

"Well, boy," said Miss Lucy, as pretty a girl as ever I hope to see, "you can't keep yourself, and you want to stay here, that's the ticket, isn't it?"

I forgot the warning and said hotly, "I want to come the day after tomorrow and will give you two pounds, and you can turn me out when they are used up," and I took the notes out of my waistcoat pocket.

She was about to say something bitter as to the purchasing power of two pounds, but checked herself. "I won't take the money before you come, but it is understood that you are looking for a job. Do you want to see your room or would you rather not," she added cynically.

"I suppose it has a roof to it," I said.

"Very well, then," she said, "the day after tomorrow, unless you think better of it." And she turned away.

"And why, you young shaver, did you tell me yesterday that you only had fifteen shillings?" asked Woodenleg.

"I suppose because I didn't know you well enough to trust you," I said, "but I assure you I haven't more than two pounds now."

"You're mighty sharp," he muttered, "but we'll see what comes of it."

"I look on you as a friend," I rejoined, "and you can believe that or not, just as you please. Good afternoon." And I made my way past him into the street, and back, after a tea of two buns, to the hotel where, much to my grief, no letter awaited me.

XIV

Looking back, I hardly know how I should have got through my early days in London but for firstly, my self-denial with regard to places of amusement, and secondly the notebook. Regarding the former as a great snare which would inevitably entrap me in the end, but which I was bound to keep at a distance as long as I could, I managed, I think, fairly well. With no opinion of my own virtues or cleverness, I had a very high one of other people's cleverness. It would, I argued, stand me in good stead to lead, for a fortnight at least, the life of a temperate student. Of course I must go to the dogs some day, but what a consolation, immediately after my school disgrace, to have succeeded even for a short period in being decent.

As for the notebook, its main purpose was to save me from contradicting myself and telling the wrong lies. I had stumbled over the two pounds and fifteen shillings with Woodenleg, so I made an entry thus:

"N.B. Staying with father at Kingsley, allows you five shillings a week. See him Sundays, when he gives you money. Always have five shillings in pocket."

To this story I adhered for some time, and it served me. I was able to give graphic, if idealized, accounts of my father to different people, some of whom would even ask me for his views on public matters. My actual interviews with him, two in number—he stayed at the York Hotel when he took up work in the Censor's Office—I will describe in their place. Yes, I have been a good son.

The notebook also contained prayers and aspirations of a vague order, which relieved my feelings for the moment, and would do me no harm, if it fell into strange hands.

XV

Two letters were on my plate next morning; I took them to my bedroom and read them attentively. My father wrote that he had received mine; he was glad that I had done the right thing in joining up; he supposed that by now I had a number; I should probably find the life hard at first. Who was my Company Officer? Would Knightsbridge Barracks find me for long? He enclosed ten shillings, and hoped I would write soon again giving more details. He was entering on his new duties on Monday. "Remember your dear mother," he ended. The second was from Hal, and read, in amended English, as follows:

"Dear Master Reginald, The wife received yours safely. The master tells us that you are in the Fighting Fifth. A parcel of clothes is being sent off for your friend

by this post with the master's consent;
also a new pair of army boots, regulation
pattern, for yourself. Please acknowledge
same. Our best wishes to you, Master
Reggie, in your new life.

> "Yours faithfully,
> "Harold Robbins."

So a parcel was coming. The third letter
was from my school friend, forwarded from
home.

> "Dear old Sport, There was a tremen-
> dous bust-up when we got back in the
> evening. Sticky called the house together
> and produced the bottle (sensation in
> court). The boy who bought this had now
> left the school. It was his wish that no one
> else should be implicated, therefore Sticky
> would ask no questions. The other cul-
> prits knew their own guilt, let them make
> amends for the disgrace they had helped
> to bring on a schoolfellow by being very
> careful how they behaved in future; this
> was their last chance. Amen. So we are
> not going to leave at the end of the term.
> The place is wretched without you. Has
> the Governor cut up rough? Write to us.
> Enclosed is a quid for the beastly bottle,

don't be proud and send it back. We love you, Reg.

"Yrs. ever J. F."

"Lis writing to you when he hears from you, he says."

I am not ashamed to think that I burst out crying. It was worth while being expelled to get a letter like that. Looking at the postmark, I saw that my friend had taken the precaution to post it some three miles from the school. If he were so shrewd as that, he would probably leave in the natural course.

How should I deal with these letters? That required thought. I passed an hour in the British Museum, and came to the conclusion that my father's had better be ignored. He was bound to find out some time that I was not in the Army, and in any case this was the last shilling I should get out of him. I was angry with Molly for not writing; Hal was clearly under my father's thumb. Should I acknowledge the boots and the clothes when they came? Should I write a letter from the imaginary receiver of the clothes? That would be amusing, but a gratuitous forgery, when once the clothes were mine. Finally, before the parcel came, I went into the Y.M.C.A. and wrote a postcard, "Boots and clothes received with many thanks; my friend is writing," and after some doubt addressed to my father and posted it on the spot.

J. F.'s I intended to leave until I was at my new address, as rather a deep scheme had suggested itself with regard to him.

I had a cheap lunch, and returned to the hotel, where I found two parcels, the boots and the clothes. The former, I reflected, would be most useful (besides, socks had been sent with them) in London, where even shoes with Phillips' rubbers must soon wear down; still, being Army clothing, I shrunk from wearing them yet awhile. I changed into the clothes, though; a flannel shirt with collar, pair of socks, and tie were included. I don't wear underclothing, so I was not so badly off for apparel, having packed some handkerchiefs in the hand-bag, with which I left school. I made a parcel of my better suit and the boots, etc., and congratulated myself on being able to appear at Marchmont Street with two pieces of luggage.

XVI

I then strolled down Charing Cross Road with the intention of turning into the National Gallery, which I had never seen. ("There are plenty of things to be seen in London, if you keep your eyes open, besides entertainments, and many of them gratis," I was always saying to myself.) Outside one of the bookshops, I ran into one of our house prefects, who had left last term, and whose sight disqualified him for the Army.

"Whatever are you doing in town in the middle of term?" he asked, before I could avoid him.

"Oh," I said casually, not looking at him, "I've been sacked."

He didn't ask why, which surprised me, but, "Are you with your people?"

"No," I said, "they've turned me out, and I'm trying to earn a living. Don't let me keep you."

He took a couple of books from under his arm and handed them to me. "Look here," he said, "I had just got these for myself, but it strikes me they will be more useful to you, if you deign to read them. Good-bye, Bolland." And he went on.

I did not know whether to throw the books at his head; they were *Tom Jones*. Still I was glad to have something, albeit dull to read when I felt restless. I don't know that I profited by the book, which I finished in about a month, but I had a great admiration for all the characters; especially the hero. There was hardly a man in real life to whom I looked up at that time, so Tom certainly filled a gap in my affections. I put off my visit to the National Gallery and saw Westminster Abbey instead.

XVII

Of my five weeks' stay in Marchmont Street I shall say little, for the very good reason that I fell in love there. Lucy, my star, will you ever know what you have been to me? By birth I am a gentleman and you a common person, yet what is that to me? You are a thousand times my better in true refinement and sympathy. Whatever I do, I shall be comforted with your image and the certainty that to you I owe the sense of what love is. I helped you, I know, perhaps when you were least aware of help. I found a man to protect you, though his protection was not disinterested. Whether you marry him eventually or break with him, I shall have no fear for you, nor in any case shall I be jealous; I never wanted you for myself, I was not greedy for you, only grateful that you gave me so much of yourself, and glad, yes glad, that you did not give me more. It must be understood then (it seems I am writing as if I expected a reader), that I am stopping at my new address whither I moved the morning after I received the parcels. The life that I describe was led outside these lodging where, besides Lucy and her mother, Woodenleg, whom I shall keep as far as possible in the background, was my sole companion.

XVIII

I had a little bedroom at the top of the house; there I wrote most of those unhappy letters that afterwards gave me the reputation of a young blackmailer. Now I am not mercenary, and the practice of living on other people's money, unless they supply it willingly, has no charm for me. It is never pleasant to threaten anyone, for threatening is a species of bully-ing, which, like every decent person, I detest. Besides I cannot order people about, though there are some whose orders I take a positive pleasure in obeying.

Now J. F.'s letter had to be answered; he liked me and wanted to hear from me. What could be more natural then, after thanking him for his amusing note and for refunding the price of the whisky (paying for it had completely slipped my memory), that I should go on to say that I was living from hand to mouth, an exciting experience, since my father, having lost his fortune, had reached the extent of good nature. I will take my oath that I coupled this statement with no request for money; oh dear no, why should I? For at the moment I was, speaking relatively, flush. I even went so far as to say that I had determined to earn my living, and had high hopes of starting shortly on the stage in quite a small way. This was not a pure lie, as will be evident. Nor, as persons have tried to make out, was there indecency in this or any of my letters. I kept Georgette out of them entirely, although I knew well enough that the seamy side of town life, described by a novice, could not fail to appeal to an athletic schoolboy like my friend.

By return of post J. F. wrote to me enclosing another pound note, entreating my acceptance of it, I must not think of repaying; if I wanted to borrow of him, he was always ready to lend up to ten pounds. I was never so much surprised in my life as by this gift, and wrote back in these terms:

"My dear J. F., Uncommonly good of you to write. Of course I would not dream of borrowing of you, for one thing, I might never be able to repay, for another, a loan would weigh heavily on my spirits, which simply must be buoyant, you understand. A gift is another thing, and as you send me a pound, for which I am really grateful, it is not likely, while I am a sane man, that I should send it back. But, my dear fellow, don't send any more. My gratitude has its limits, if your generosity hasn't. Let this be the beginning and end of my unemployment pay, or I will not write to you again. You will do me a real favour by sending Jacoby's address; I meant to ask for it in my last. Love to L. and the fags.

"Yours,
"R. B."

But for one phrase in this letter perhaps I should be good friends with my aunt today, counsel with L. Wags both of them, they agreed that I was unlikely to earn anything as long as I lived, and that it would be a great joke to send me £1 fortnightly (which they could well afford, their fathers, who have since got hold of my side of the correspondence, being partners in the timber trade) in future. Accordingly, a month later, two pound notes arrived, pinned to a sheet of paper, on which was written, "Unemployment Pay. Please acknowledge." Really angry, I returned them without a word of explanation. Back they came with "Take it, don't be an idiot." I did what anybody else would have done, and from that time made it a rule never to refuse money, when offered.

XIX

It might be expected that a young man about to earn his living would have recourse to an employment bureau, even if stress of circumstances did not drive him to apply at an establishment where "Boy wanted" was stuck up in the window; but Woodenleg dropped a remark, not to me, at breakfast one morning, which proved how useless it is for a gentleman's son to attempt any thing in these channels. Even if I got a job, it would very soon be made clear that I was not the man they wanted, indeed, whatever may have been the case in past days, there is no doubt that under class prejudice today it is we who suffer, not the poor.

In point of fact I disbelieved what I heard, and went to an employment bureau, where I waited my turn patiently. What applicants! Broken, wounded men, labourers who had steered clear of military service, a young jailbird, hardly older than I, who had done his three months for demanding money with threats at a post office. In front of me stood a fellow of about thirty-two, a boot-maker I thought from his sharp downward glancing eyes, wearing a ragged coat and trousers, but fashionable moccasins. Two or three were sent off to jobs at once, the rest left their names and addresses. I was met with a quizzical stare and asked if I had any experience of any trade. I said I could add up figures. "Can you drive a car?" I said no. I gave my age as just under eighteen and came away. Outside I was stopped by a man in plain clothes, who asked me if my name was Roderick Ames. I said no, who was he? "A young man who'd better be careful, not you, sir." Completely mystified I went on to Georgette.

The door was opened by a tall lanky man with yellow hair and a straggling moustache, who looked at me kindly when I gave my name. Georgette was clearly annoyed at my entry, as I had interrupted a *tête-à-tête*. "Have you a job yet?" she asked. I told her where I had just been, and Mr. Castle (he afterwards introduced himself) said he admired my pluck. He seemed to be one of that large class, who, by a combination of indifferent health, charming manners, and extravagance, succeeded in passing through the war without doing any public work. He mentioned many actors and artists and asked if I were an artist. I said no, but added that I liked pictures, whereupon he gave me a ticket for a show of modem decorative work in a Bond Street gallery on the following day.

I was encouraged by this attention to ask him the quickest way to get on the stage. He said he had always heard that the chorus of a musical comedy afforded the best training in gesture, though most people would recommend a dramatic school.

"He has quarrelled with his father," broke in Georgette.

Mr. Castle hoped that the quarrel was not permanent.

"But how," I asked, "do I get into a musical comedy chorus?"

"Shall we advise him to hang round stage doors?" he laughed to Georgette.

"I think," she said, "that he ought to be made to work with his hands."

"Needlework!" I exclaimed, at which they both laughed, I could not in the least see why.

"Where are you lodging?" asked Georgette.

I described the house and its inmates, and Mr. Castle said he enjoyed the society of that kind of people; did I think he could come to a meal? I said I had not been with them very long, and, as I might not be able to pay the bill eventually, I hardly liked to take the risk of springing strangers on them, although I was sure they would amuse him.

Georgette was giving me hints to go all this while, so, not wishing to lose my footing there, I excused myself on the ground that I was going to look at the statues in the Museum. Mr. Castle saw me out, and advised me not to miss the show tomorrow afternoon. I went back to Marchmont Street.

XX

Woodenleg was rather a pathetic character, a sort of decayed literary amateur. His parentage was mixed; of German descent, he seemed unable to do anything in a straightforward English way. For instance, instead of telling me that I was a liar in money matters, he would be continually saying, "Bolland has strange ideas about money," not in a captious or defamatory tone, but as a piece of natural history. Again, when he was accused of living on the widow of an artist who had been killed in the war, he did not lose his temper, but muttered, "She was very kind to me, my friends are very kind to me," in a moody complacent grunt. He wanted someone he might superintend and advise after a paternal fashion. He made no impression whatever on Miss Lucy, who sent him about his business almost rudely. I was more amenable, so found myself treated to tirades against publishers and editors of reviews, who for the last twenty years had returned his contributions. He had a scrap-book, containing the few articles that had appeared in print and notices of him; this was produced in the evening, and he would give us elegant extracts to show that he really was an unappreciated genius and an honour to any house in which he took up his abode. Many of the articles were what are known, I believe, as "turnovers," essays on various subjects wide asunder as the poles, "Summer", "Whales and Sharks", "The Origin of Conundrums"; the notices dealt with him in the role of reciter, and were grossly flattering, as his voice was raucous. However, I feel a cad to run him down; he gave me many a straight tip about human nature. To hear him talk about some of the good characters he had met on his journey (he had a great belief in goodness) was a moral education, because you knew the people were real. Oddly enough this power quite deserted him when he set pen to paper; everything I saw of his was dull as ditchwater.

He told me that the man who gave me *Tom Jones* was a good friend, and when I said I hardly knew him and had not exchanged a hundred words with him at school, because I

was not his fag, he said that made no difference, and it was quite possible never to have
seen one's best friend. Of course he was thinking of people in America and the Colonies
reading what he wrote and liking it.

He was standing outside the house, his
habit of an afternoon, when I returned, and,
hearing of the exhibition of decorative work,
burst into a sudden fury, which, I thought at
first, was assumed in order to show off his critical abilities to anyone who might be passing.

"Decorative!" he roared, "that's all they
think of nowadays, not honest work, not
beautiful work, not the work of a lifetime, but
decorative work!"

"I see nothing wrong in the word 'decorative'," I ventured to suggest, "in fact it strikes
me as sensible and expressive of modem
tendencies."

"So that's the jargon you are picking up.
Who are your new friends, eh?"

Before I could answer, he went on,
"Modem tendencies, indeed! That every dis-
eased notion that crosses a scatter-brained
numbskull should be registered in paint and
served up for the pleasure of a few hysterical
women and invertebrate youths! You'll do for
yourself presently, my fine friend. Do you
know that there are hundreds of artists who

have worked patiently for ten, twenty, thirty years, and cannot get their work shown, while these empty noddles throw off a dozen smears and scratches and call it Venus Anadyomene, put it into the garden to dry, and, bless you, it's sold before it is exhibited."

"What do you mean by saying that I'll do for myself?" I asked.

"What do I mean?" he growled, looking at me very suspiciously; "you'll find out soon enough." He turned and stumped into the house. Unwilling to pursue him with questions, I walked westward to a theatre, getting something to eat on the way.

I was in any case too late for the piece, but I lounged outside the stage door as if I were waiting for somebody. One or two passers-by thought they recognized me, but discovered they were in error. Soon the actors and actresses came out; the stars did not interest me; I wanted to observe the small fry. They looked half starved and shifty, but there was an appealing friendliness about them. A red-haired girl with a parcel under her arm asked me if I was waiting for anyone. I said no, but I wanted to get an idea of what stage life was like. "Keep off it," she said; "it will neither pay nor serve you. It is one long tiresome drift, but when you've begun with it, you have to keep on; why, I can't explain, but so it is." Inquisitiveness spoiled this encounter, for I began to ask her about the parts she had played; she at once drew in her horns, probably regretting having spoken her mind to me. I said "Thank you," raised my hat, and walked on to another theatre. Here I took up a bolder attitude. Approaching a young fellow issuing from the stage door, I said, "Excuse me, sir" (young people like to be sir'd), "I feel I must tell you how much I enjoyed your acting; I am not a journalist, just a private individual." He seemed rather nonplussed, and faltered that he was glad. Nothing more came of that. Still unsatisfied, I went on to a third theatre, but it was too late.

I walked back to supper, told them that I was trying like anything to be an actor, that I had not exhausted a quarter of the theatres yet, but decided privately to give up the idea of the stage, having an inkling that I should "find myself" before very long in some pleasant idle capacity. I did not give up my folly of frequenting stage doors, which led me to rather remarkable company in the long run. At present I had not the key of the front door, so could not let myself in late at night; it was given me after a fortnight.

XXI

I wore my boots next day, as my shoes began to show signs of wear. Every day I made a point of taking exercise in the morning, as I was in fear of losing my healthy complexion. I did not always go in one of the parks, but more often chose poor streets, to accustom myself to squalid surroundings, because I had made up my mind to feel for the poor always.

The show in the afternoon was delightful. To my surprise Mr. Castle was there with a party of two women and a rather slackly dressed youth with long hair. I smiled to him at a distance, but did not intrude myself. He came across to me, which I thought nice of him, gave me a catalogue, and told me what to admire. As I was leaving the gallery, he stopped me, asking if I had an engagement for tea. I said I was going back to Marchmont Street, but he invited me to his rooms in St.

James' Street, where he would join me in a few minutes. He was as good as his word.

The flat was of the newest style, a smattering of Chinese ornament and a great deal of black. We sat on a divan, and drank our tea (Russian of course) from cups without handles. He asked me how long I had known Georgette, and I told him the truth. "Is she dependable?" I asked.

"I don't quite know what you mean," he replied, "but she is not jealous."

"Do you think she cares for me?" I asked. "I have so few friends in London, and one likes to be certain of them."

"Make yourself easy," he laughed (I didn't like his laugh, it wasn't hearty); "she gave me a message for you: will you go on to supper with her when you leave here—the supper is my affair by the way. I wish I could be with you, but I promised to dine with a man and his wife."

I told him there was a difficulty about my getting back late at night, but he said they would not lock up before half past ten.

"You would think," he said, in answer to my admiration of his pictures, "that I have all I want, but that is not so—the woman is absent; a house, however small, without a woman is a misnomer."

I was not quite certain that they meant anything, so asked him directly why he liked Georgette. "For many reasons," he said. "First, because she is so modern; you have no idea how modern. I don't think there is a single illicit relationship that she will not countenance; with her it is '*tout comprendre*'. For instance, she does not rule out passion in friendships between men; what is your view?"

I was not going to disagree with him, so I mumbled something like "Charity covers a multitude of sins", and he squeezed the nape of my neck quite gently.

"I did not introduce you to my party in the gallery," he went on, "because they might have off ended you by their outspokenness; they are of the modem persuasion, and have no sympathy with Victorian conventions."

"Nothing offends me," I shouted.

"You are right," he said, and then pensively, "it takes a lot of people to make a world." Apologizing if I bored him, I proceeded with my troubles, telling him, with as much humour as I could command, about my prowls round the theatres. He chuckled, and asked if I could paint or write. "I have absolutely no creative talent whatever," I said.

"Nevertheless," he rejoined, "I think in Paris you would be called an artist, and other artists would club together to enable you to live for art." He looked at me as if he meant this. Rightly or wrongly I affected to take his words at surface value only, and said, "Paris is not London."

"I don't know," he said; "we have some artists yet amongst us, and many connoisseurs. Have a liqueur." I was already smoking one of his scented cigarettes, and declined, feeling that I might be drugged, but at last I consented to swallow the mixture. He drew the curtains and lit a joss-stick, as he said, to drive out the fog, though I was not aware of any. I was now lying at full length on the divan, when I caught sight of my boots, and made an effort to remove them (all the time I was afraid of off ending him), saying that I hoped I had not dirtied the material.

"You have the instincts of an artist," he said, and offered to unlace them. I took my feet off the divan, and in a muddleheaded way explained that I was saving my shoes.

"I will get you a pair of shoes," he said.

"I am afraid," I said, "that you will never speak to me again, coming into your rooms and sprawling about like a Bolshevist."

"On the contrary," he said, "you are always welcome here, remember that. I have no spare bedroom, or I would offer it you. Don't go yet; Georgette doesn't expect you till seven."

At this point, probably thanks to the liqueur, I broke down. "Mr. Castle," I said, "I am ashamed of myself, let me go." I staggered up and fell against him. He put his arm round my waist and sat down with me on the divan.

"Why did you ask me here?" I cried. "I have only made a fool of myself."

"I asked you here" (I expected he would say this) "to help you. You must not blame yourself or do anything rash. You could not help coming; it is the luckiest thing in the world, and you will come again." He wrote his telephone number on a card and gave it me, not asking my address, but I remembered afterwards that Georgette had it. He took me into his bedroom, where I washed, and sent me out. Hating and congratulating myself, I made my way to Jermyn Street, where a new surprise awaited me.

XXII

Georgette was in evening dress, wearing a
string of beautiful pearls, she was not painted,
but her hair was dressed to perfection; a shawl
floated round her shoulders. "Ah," she cried,
admitting me, "it's pretty Bollond."

"Oh," I said, "I am in filthy rags; I must go
away again."

"Of course not, you little gentleman," she
exclaimed; "come in!"

"I can't in these clothes."

"Take them off, then." She laughed, and
drew me through the doorway, then began
unbuttoning my waistcoat. I did not know
what to do, blushing and squirming. She
was in earnest, and reproached me for not
feeling honoured by her proposal. I begged,
if I undressed, to have some covering to
avoid catching cold. She remarked that there
was a fire, and offered me her shawl. "Don't

you know, you monster," she went on, as I obeyed, with my eye on the salmon, pheasant and champagne bottle, "that you have stolen Freddy Castle's heart; I never knew he owned such a thing till you came on the scene."

"I am very sorry," I said, "but I am not what you think me; I don't mean mischief."

"I don't care what you mean," she said, "it's what you've done. Ever since you dropped in yesterday afternoon he can talk of nothing else. It's very hard on me, it is really; I was so sure of him." By this time I was entirely stripped and clumsily endeavouring to drape myself. She told me to open the champagne, while she dispensed the fish. "*Pity* Bollond," I said, quite naturally, so she gave me an eider-down. "I'll go away, I will really," I added; "I can't afford to make trouble or mischief, have my living to think of."

"You can't help it," she said, "nor can he, nor can I."

"That's all very well, but it's awkward, and my physical removal simplifies matters. Come, a glass of fiz! Your best, Georgette, and believe me, I'll never stand in your way."

"What does it matter?" she said, raising her glass. "I'll beat you."

"You won't, if you challenge me."

"I didn't mean that," she said. "Will you do something to please me tonight?"

"Haven't I done enough?" I said, pointing to the eiderdown.

"Carve the bird." She had me there, I admit. Well—we ate and drank, and I became sorrowful, peevishly regretting the past, until she asked me if I thought she would ever get married.

"Not to Mr. Castle."

"Why do you say that?"

"You're not his type."

"What is his type?"

I thought of Lucy and held my tongue a minute. "Do you think I shall get on all right in London? I'm on the make like everyone else."

"Pour yourself out some more to drink."

By the time we had finished the raspberry jelly I was affectionate and had my head in her lap. She said I might lie in her bed if I felt cold. It was now a pleasure to do so, and she lay beside me. How I kissed her hair! We gratified each other completely before it was time for me to go, but I was not quite open with her because of my forethought for Lucy, whom even then I liked to consider as the princess of the St. James' Street flat. Had I only held myself in view, I could not have won so much enjoyment from what was after all a vulgar evening. The champagne did not disturb my balance like the liqueur, and when I got into the open air the effects had worn off. I was only a little flushed when I reached home, full of beneficent intentions towards the world and good hopes for the future. There was only one disadvantage; I had lost the card which until now I took for the ace of trumps, my bodily innocence.

XXIII

The looking-glass showed no difference in my face. I expected a knowing look to appear in my eyes in the course of the next few days, but no; I gave up watching for it after three weeks.

I have spoken of a deep scheme with regard to J. F. It was this. There was a fellow in our house called Jacoby, who left two terms after I came. He was an original man, and I liked fagging for him; he never caned me, though he would have liked to have done so. I interested him. He said once that I was cut out for a life of adventure. He came down once or twice after he went to Cambridge, and took me out. I knew he had been wounded in the war and heard that he had got work in a Government office. He was well off, and I thought, if he were living alone, he might not only be glad to see me, but we might arrange to live together; of course he might have lost interest in me.

Now J. F. heard occasionally from him, for, unlike most scholars, he kept in with the athletic set, preferring them to prefects. Imagine my joy therefore at receiving an answer from J. F. saying that Jacoby was living at an address in Maida Vale, was bored with life and glad to see me at any time; I was almost sure to find him in between tea and dinner, if I made no appointment.

I did not trust Mr. Castle across the road; the impression I had made on him might vanish in a week, when he might pass me without recognition. He wanted a charming woman to keep house for him, and here I could serve him. His affectations and sloppiness contrasted favourably with Lucy's downright petulance; they might make a pair, for she was desperate to obtain a settled position in the world, which I could certainly not give her. She was too manly, and he too womanly; yes, in a workaday world theirs would be a charming companionship. An opportunity was wanted to bring them together, which came about quite unexpectedly in a very short time.

But I had to think of myself. Schemes for other people's happiness generally result in a reckless waste of mental energy with no real satisfaction. I would call on Jacoby that day.

XXIV

The house in Maida Vale was externally almost
as dingy as the Marchmont Street lodgings,
which were promised a coating of paint in the
spring, but inside, what a difference! A neat
maid opened the door, and showed me through
a hall, wainscoted in oak, into a library, where
a wood fire was burning. Jacoby was out, but
expected back before the hour. It was the
room of a student with one eye on modern
life. Classical authors leant on low shelves to
the right of the hearth; first editions of the
Yellow Book, some Kelmscotts and Chiswick
Press books, in what must have been once a
china cupboard (the shelves were so broad) in
the middle of the wall, facing a shabby back
garden. On the large centre table was a fern,
some French novels, and a new fashion-paper.
A set of Walter Pater's works stood on the bureau; Jacoby was reading *Marius*.

I looked at my nails, and dusted my boots with my handkerchief. Clearly I must be spick and span in this house; that struck me as curious. With Mr. Castle I did not feel that sense of respect; a survival, I suppose, of one's deference to prefects.

I had not to wait long for Jacoby, who seemed extremely depressed, and did not share the general feeling of tiptoe expectation with regard to the settlement of the war. I suppose he had seen so much monotony in the trenches and War Office that he was inured.

"Glad to see you, Bollond," was his greeting. "Extended leave from school?"

The remark was so strained and unlike him that I was perplexed. "Hasn't J. F. told you about my mishap! I hope so, as I don't like telling people myself," I said. At once I saw that he was testing me, the kind of literary thing he would do. "No," I went on, "my hand isn't against society. I don't consider that I've been ill treated in the least—in fact, if I had a son, I should act towards him exactly in my father's way, were he guilty of the same behaviour."

"Where are you staying," he asked, "and are you in London for long?"

I told him my address and my difficulties with regard to a profession.

"You'd make a good actor," he said, "but it's hard to get on. I can put you up here at most times, you know."

"The worst of this place," I said, looking round me, "is that once in, I should never want to get out; it's paradise to where I'm living."

"You'd come for a month?" he said.

"You're very kind. I'd give you a week's warning, but I'm keeping you now. You're dining out?" He said he had to meet a man at the Marble Arch at half past seven, and suggested that we might go along together. So I sat down again. He told me that the house was his mother's, she also had a cottage at Pevensey Bay, but preferred to live at hotels. He described her vividly, not quite as a son should, as a fashionable seeker after novelties of every kind. She took a china cat about with her wherever she went, and the mantelpiece of her private sitting-room (she always stayed on the first floor) had to be cleared entirely for its reception; there it stood, a green fetish with a pink chiffon bow round its neck. She followed the newest phases of modern thought feverishly, and in her letters demanded what was positively the last philosophy; he said he had told her three times Universal Suicide, but she continued to ask. I thought his taking in the fashion paper rather in her style, though I did not say so.

"You must meet Mother," he ended up, "you would amuse her. *Sans penser, sans rester,* that is her motto. She had a bookplate designed of a wave with that written across it, a hideous thing. You get on with women, don't you?"

"I never know whether they are laughing at me."

"Depend upon it they are not, if you feel like that. They don't like me, they think I am laughing at them, well—so I am in a sort of way; their abject triviality tickles my sense of humour."

"What you say about triviality," I said very gravely, not quite certain if I was going to be absurd, "is true, but don't you think everything is trivial, if you keep on at it long enough?"

"Possibly, but what has that to do with women?"

"I mean, but I can't express it properly, that their aimless fussing about twopenny-halfpenny things, one after another, works out the same, pretty much, as man's long persistence in one great object."

"I suppose so," he murmured, putting his fingers through his hair. "I wish I knew what I was going to do after the war."

"You feel you ought to make a living, even if you've got one."

"Ah!" he cried, as if waking up, "you have touched the twentieth-century problem; more of that when you come to stay. We must be going."

He talked to me in a cynical world-weary manner until we parted, but he looked considerably brighter. The way to get on with him was to draw him up on his pedestal to air his views, saying as little as possible one's self. "I must keep in with Jacoby," I repeated quietly all the way back, "make myself indispensable to him; who knows what may come of it?"

XXV

I was mistaken, however, in my view of Mr. Castle; he had taken a real fancy to me. I forgot to say that I mentioned him to Jacoby, who looked up rather queerly and said, "Friend of yours?" in the same forced tone as "Extended leave". I said I knew him slightly that was all. "No one knows much about him," said Jacoby, "except that he's fabulously rich, there's no doubt about that, and is running a newspaper, said to be the last word on art; Mother was asking about it the other day. The first number's not out yet. Are his people the ginger-beer firm?" I saw him several times before Armistice Day, when he was most affectionate, and bought me the shoes. The Marchmont Street household, except Lucy's mother, went in a party to Buckingham Palace to hear the news proclaimed, but I managed to lose them in Charing Cross Road, which was not difficult, and went on by appointment to St. James' Street, where Mr. Castle and I hung flags. He dressed me up in a Union Jack, and declared that Slobatcher should paint me as England, for his set of national fantasias; a boy Britannia would be such a stark idea. He told me a lot about *Fire*, which was coming out next day. Fresh talent was badly wanted; he did not mean to puff the circulation by the old method of leading lights; in the first number the only well-known contributor was Minnicote, and he only had a dozen lines on a back page. Did I know of any artist or writer whose work might be suitable?

Thinking to do a friend a turn, I told him about Woodenleg, what a strange person he was; I didn't see anything in his writing, but I was no judge of course; Mr. Castle would know at once.

So late in the afternoon (we had a sumptuous lunch at the Piccadilly) we went back to Marchmont Street, and the first move was made in my project for Lucy's happiness. She struck him as not only beautiful, but refined, and he kept on saying afterwards, "What a face for the stage!" Some days later she confided to me that she was casting about for a part. I told Mr. Castle, and that is how she got a repertory engagement.

Woodenleg amused him, as did her exploiting of him; he took away some specimens of his work. Next day I had been asked to lunch at Princes to meet Bream, the author of *Poniatowski*, an historical drama based on a novel, that was going to take London by storm. As the Party was one of the most amusing I have known, I will be particular in my account.

We were eight; Bream, his wife, Miriam Grayson, Herbert Sillery, Vera Slobatcher (the artist's daughter), Georgette Masman, Mr. Castle, and I. Bream, who stood the lunch, was a pushing red-faced man, with dirty nails and a loud voice. In my small experience there are two classes of literary men, the modest and the conceited. The latter are of two kinds: either they talk of nothing but their own work, or they talk of everything but their own work, as if they had complete disposal of it. Bream was of this sort; he did not mention his play or books, except in answer to direct questions, but on politics, art criticism, actors and actresses, and of course the money market, he was ultimate.

His wife was a little sharp-featured woman, not in the least vulgar, who seemed permanently afraid that her husband might explode. "Yes, John, no, John" was the staple of her conversation, and if her neighbour addressed a remark to her, she replied nervously, turning her head away after a word, as if she were failing in her loyalty to John by not watching him all the time. She was dressed in black with white cuffs, and wore a gold and platinum chain with lapis lazuli.

Miriam Grayson, who sat on one side of Bream, was an actress—she was to play the lead in *Poniatowski*, but struck at the last moment because a half a dozen lines of her part had to be scrapped. She had a dreamy inspired look, implying that she was only an intellectual creature, not flesh and blood.

Next to her was Sillery, a gay man of the world, who would have been much more at home with a chorus girl. Vera Slobatcher I liked; she spoke English very badly, ate with relish, and seemed to be laughing at the people all the time. We had a race over almonds and raisins, which she won. She told me I was like a Russian; I believe I pinched her. I was surprised to see Georgette, who sat between Mr. Castle and Bream, but I gathered that she went everywhere in theatrical circles, and was often consulted on questions of modern dress, though she was not a milliner. She hardly took any notice of me, but Mrs. Bream did; she said she liked to see young people enjoying themselves, as she and her husband had no children of their own.

By the entrée we, that is Bream, had agreed that in five years England would be a syndicalist state. Vera asked me what that meant; I said she ought to know.

"Ah, you do not understand Russia."

"You said I was like a Russian."

"You are a fool."

"So that's the resemblance."

At which she threw an olive at me, which missed and fell into Mrs. Bream's empty glass. This was preparatory to our drinking to the success of the play.

"Tell me, Mr. Bream," enquired Miss Grayson, when the buzz subsided, "do you work out your plays on a miniature stage? Bannatyne Spink always uses one."

Mrs. Bream leant forward, before he could reply, with "John never discusses his technique with anyone."

"How disappointing!" said Miss Grayson, raising her voice sneeringly, "but of course all the German dramatists would admit that you were right."

There was an ugly pause, during which only my laughter could be heard.

"Look at that boy!" said Georgette. "What has amused him?" for I was quite red in the face.

"It's all your fault," I said, turning to Vera.

"Is he mad?" said she.

Miss Grayson turned round to Sillery and said, "I like giggling boys; so English!"

He endeavoured to pacify her by adverting to the splendid notices of her acting in the illustrated papers.

"Excuse me," I said to Mrs. Bream, recovering, "but I was reminded of an anecdote of my father, who was once mistaken for a Dutch comedian when travelling on the Continent."

My character as a serious person was established at once, and Miss Grayson asked me to tea before we broke up. Mr. Castle looked bored all the time, as well he might be, stuck between Georgette, who for some reason was exceedingly glum, and Mrs. Bream, who was not concerned with anyone but the great man. Afterwards he confessed to me that he was thinking of Lucy, and would have no peace of mind until he had seen her comfortably launched. Indeed he did not lunch or dine out for a fortnight after this party. I had a letter from him that morning, quite pathetic in its earnestness, in which he said there was one kind of beauty that struck one down like an illness, that was Lucy's; he relied on me to put no obstacles in his path; he was sending her and her mother tickets for the matinée.

XXVI

Possibly as a retribution for taking his name in vain I walked straight into my father as we left the restaurant. "I thought you were in the Army," he said.

"Demobilized this morning," said I. This was little short of an inspiration, and could only be due to the fact that I was going on to tea with one of our most charming actresses.

"You haven't been long about it."

"They took us one of the first, sir, and raw recruits first of all."

"And what do you propose to do now?"

"I am at the moment obtaining stage experience." This sounded lame, I admit, but I could not keep the flag flying long.

"You should have made some effort to stay in the Army," he said thoughtfully.

"Will you excuse me now?" I whispered. "I mustn't leave these people, they may be of use to me."

"Where are you living?"

"I will come and see you tomorrow afternoon and tell you all my news," I exclaimed in feverish impatience to escape from him.

"Very well," he grunted, "be at the Censor's Office—you know where that is—" (I nodded) "at five."

"I will most certainly," I said, and he went on. I rejoined my friends a little ahead.

"Who was that?" asked Mr. Castle, "he seemed to take an interest in you."

"My father," I remarked casually, "he is working in the Censor's Office; didn't you notice the resemblance?"

He was enormously impressed, unless he thought I was lying, and didn't want me to know. The others had observed my father, for Vera said, "You have a lot of friends in London, then?" and I had to explain once more. Miss Grayson asked me if I would mind going with her to a couple of shops first, as she had to try on a hat. I answered "No" in a tone that indicated I would follow her to the end of the world.

XXVII

The net result of that tea-party was the knowledge that I had taken tea with Miss Miriam Grayson and friend, a not yet demobilized officer, whose name is of importance to his country. As for making any further advance towards a part (I have already explained that I did not want one, but I played the young aspirant with conviction wherever I went), I can safely say that the reverse was the case, as it was made plain to me that it was of far more real importance to pass an afternoon in the company of such an artist than to play any part, short of *jeune premier*, in a production where she appeared.

I returned to Marchmont Street in a high state of excitement; Lucy thought I had been drinking. She now looked more lovely than ever. To test her feelings for me I asked her to lend me something, pretending that I was hard up. She refused; I now knew for certain that she was ignorant of my love. She confided to me next morning that she was calling on Hemingway in hopes of obtaining a part. I knew something of Hemingway's reputation for dilatoriness, so after an interview with him I took her on to Mr. Castle; she needed some persuasion. I told her that if in this matter she would be ruled by me, she might not only get a part but a man—possibly a husband, if she played her cards properly, who would give her an excellent time and introduce her right and left into the bargain.

The scene in his flat I prefer not to describe; it was painful to me. I had to connive at the sale of the girl I loved to a man who had one mistress that I knew. Lucy was promised a part at once, and given ten pounds earnest money. It was some months before they lived together in the flat. How Georgette was squared I do not know; she has not troubled them, and I have only seen her once or twice since, when she made no reference to Lucy. Mr. Castle said he was eternally my debtor in this matter, and I have had recourse to him more than once when my funds were low. If the case, in which I am called as a witness, should result in my prosecution, he would cheerfully finance the defence. He gives me a dinner now and again, and has promised me stalls for pieces in which Lucy is playing.

I met my father outside his office at five; he seemed fairly cheerful. "You young villain," he began. "I don't believe you've been in the Army at all."

"You've only my word for it, sir."

"I suppose your discharge is being sent after you."

"Exactly."

"That was a fine woman in your party yesterday."

"I had tea with her; I don't know if it will lead to anything—" he stared at me, "—in a professional way, I mean."

"I don't like to think of a son of mine being on the stage," he said, "but as long as you keep decent company and regular hours, I suppose it is as safe a profession as most."

We walked to his club, where he gave me tea. I asked after Hal and Molly; he said they were looking for small farm in Sussex, Hal's county, but he did not know their address. Our house was up for auction next month. I think he was pleased that I did not ask for money. It was difficult to maintain an independent attitude, but I don't think I was subservient. I told him a great deal about Marchmont Street, never mentioned Jacoby, and pretended that the West End had small fascination for me. I added (this was a sudden afterthought) that I had been to a labour bureau that day (accurately describing my real attempt), as I thought one could not have too many irons in the fire. Altogether I satisfied him, and he told me to come and see him when I had a job; the club always found him; he was uncertain how long he would be stopping at the York. I little thought when I came away that this was the last time I should talk to him.

XXVIII

I have come to the last page but one of my exercise book, and Dorothy has written that she will be here this afternoon. Shall I write any more when she comes? Shall I show her this? Shall I tell her about Lucy? These are questions to be considered. What a quiet week I have spent, seeing no one but Jacoby's old nurse, avoiding Eastbourne entirely! Thank goodness my eyes are rested by the writing habit! I am calmer too in mind, for, knowing exactly what my past life has been, I shall face the court with considerable assurance. It is extraordinary how I have been able to remember details and the connected order of events. Yes, I must go on with this account at all costs, if only to see where my memory breaks down. I will walk round to the stationer's at once for two more exercise books.

XXIX

Little of importance happened during the next fortnight, at the end of which I left Marchmont Street, except my first meeting with Ames. I was strolling outside a stage door, when a voice said, "Waiting for somebody?" I looked round and saw a smartly-dressed young fellow, slightly taller than I, wearing a bowler. A man about town, I thought, not an actor. "No," I said; but he cut off my explanation with "Come and have a drink." We went to a bar in Shaftesbury Avenue, and I told him my name. I said Reginald, for it was quite impossible to lie to him; he made me feel ashamed of cowardice and lying. "Having a weekend in town?" he asked. I said I had left school, and was casting about how to live. "We'll go on to my rooms after this, if you've no objection," said he, "perhaps I can put you in the way of something." I said I was not pressed for time. He paid for my drink, and we walked to Shepherd's Market, he explaining how he found that he got more out of life by living quite cheaply as far as rooms went.

He knew the cost of lodgings in most parts of London and compared them. He had a single room on the first floor, in great disorder. The bed was not made, nor was breakfast cleared away, evening dress and white waistcoat were lying on a chair, a forage cap and tunic hung from the door, a swagger cane and riding-switch were on the mantelpiece in front of a dirty mirror. He took off his hat and sat on the bed, eyeing me humorously. "Well, Reggie Bollond, how would you like to be one of Roderick Ames' boys? There's motor-stealing now; I can introduce you to 'Red', how would you like that? No good? All for the Gaiety chorus? Let's see you walk— walk! I mean it, from where you're standing to the fireplace."

I felt I would do everything this man told me.

"That's far too fast! Why, no one can see you, you don't give them time. Shorter steps! That's better; turn your toes in more, don't hold your head so high. Look at the middle of the back in front of you, as you walk down the street; remember that in future. Do the same bit of the room six times as I told you; head's still too high. You don't mind, do you?"

"Not a bit," I said, as I obeyed him; "but where does all this lead to?" He considered me. "Yes, I think you're perfect enough, unless you go and forget it all as soon as you get outside. Come and sit down by me now, and I'll tell you where it leads to."

"Are you Roderick Ames?"' I asked.

"That's my name," he said, "and there's many a boy who's glad he fell in with me. You're not unlike me, you know."

Looking at him, I saw that he was right; his face was rounder than mine and more evil, but he had the same cast of features.

"I'll get into bed; I'm deadly tired. I was dancing till six o'clock this morning. Don't go away, unless you want to." He undressed, and took a letter out of his coat as he put it over a chair. "Read that," he said, handing it me. It was a prostrate avowal of gratitude in four pages from some wretched youth of the people whom he had befriended. I sat reading it on the bed. "You can blush, I see," was his comment when I handed it back. I asked what he had done for the fellow. "Only put him on the right path, as I will you—but I don't expect you'll write to me like that. Come closer" (he was now in bed) "and I'll tell you what you are."

"I'd rather not hear."

"You're an out-and-out boy, never care for anybody, thinking that everybody cares for you."

"That's quite untrue," I shouted. "I don't care for *you*, if that's what you mean, and now I'm going."

"All serene," he said, turning on his side; "you'll soon come back again."

"That may very well be," I replied, "but I'm going now, anyhow. Shall I turn down the light? No? Then good-bye." He did not answer and I went away.

XXX

Dorothy insists that I met her that evening as I came from him. I am sure that it was fully a month later when I was staying with Jacoby, with whom I now corresponded. It was a timid letter I sent him, describing myself as a person of unobtrusive ways and noiseless habits, though he might well have formed an adequate opinion of me from our meeting.

Ames, I think, had made me frightened of myself; his was the one personality which so far had mastered me. I felt he was more necessary to me than I to him, that, in fact, I was driven to him, "could not help coming", as Mr. Castle had said, when I entered his flat, though that was not so. I walked as he told me, quite against my better judgment, and found people staring at me in the streets; still I persisted. I gave my father a wide berth, writing to him (not on postcards, as I did when I first left home) in a vague way that suggested I was understudying in a piece that followed *Poniatowski*. Jacoby wrote back that I was welcome on the day I proposed; he intended me to take a course of reading, as he hoped to make a literary man of me, unless I was very much averse to the idea. I called on him once before I moved in, and he gave me *Miscellaneous Studies*, which I took away with me. I am bound to say that I preferred *Tom Jones*. However, Walter Pater somehow fitted in with my walking lesson; in either case I had to bend my will to a principle which I disliked, so that I no longer had full command of myself. I began to lose touch with reality. It occurred to me that I was an exceptional and rather interesting character, repaying study. My teeth were regular, hardly one was stopped. I rinsed them twice a day with milk of magnesia besides brushing. Thank God I did not peroxide my hair, which was not so light as I should have desired. At school all scented washes, greases and powders were strictly forbidden, but now I did not see why I should not swim in them. I polished my shoes myself, till the toe-caps shone like stars, and persuaded Mr. Castle to give me one or two of his silk handkerchiefs, in which he indulged pretty freely. He added some ties of an extravagant pattern, and an old Algerian dressing-gown, rather frayed at the sleeves, but otherwise decent. He lent me a fitted suit-case, with half the bottles missing, and a furred greatcoat, much too big for me. In this panoply I arrived at Maida Vale, meaning to stop there as long as possible.

XXXI

Jacoby burst out laughing when he saw me, and asked when I was going to take those things back to the pawnshop. With perfect control I said very quietly that I was sorry if my appearance gave offence, but I had to think of warmth. "You're hot stuff, you mean," he said; but I professed not to understand him. For the first day or two he treated my clothes as a joke, in which I carefully humoured him, then he forgot clean about them, or pretended to do so. It did not take long to discover that he had no idea what to make of his life. He was out from ten-thirty to five-thirty every day except Sundays, and no doubt did his official work well; he would come back sulky and frowning.

It was my business to see that tea was made and his slippers warm; I also had to tell him what I had read during his absence, for it was understood that I put in four hours' solid reading while he was at the office. Lying did not always serve me; he was a shrewd observer, and would find you out in a moment. For example he started me on *The Symbolist Movement in Literature*; I was to read the introduction and two of the essays, making notes if I liked. I read for about an hour after he had gone, then slept, letting the fire out, till lunch, which I always took there. In the afternoon I walked round to Georgette and found her out. I was back in time for tea, when he asked me what I had done. I said I had been reading what he told me all the time. To my surprise he asked me questions, and I confused Gérard de Nerval with some other chap, a terrible sin in his eyes. I was overcome with confusion, and said I had probably stewed over the book too long; he did not go to the length of calling me a liar to my face. I was more studious in future; besides, the book became interesting.

After four days I wrote my first poem; it was called "Homage to London Girls" and was full of hysterical emotion. Jacoby said he liked it, though it was immature, so I produced another, more regular in sentiment and form, and called it "The Dead Magician". It was about a man who saw through everybody and was loved in consequence; Jacoby said it proved me a cynic. Nothing daunted, I started on a third of great length and vigour, "Tyrannous Youth". The idea was that Youth wanted everything (everything was of course described in about 100 lines), then followed a passage showing how Youth got everything, in imagination, that is, and pined like Alexander having no more worlds to conquer, then came suicide and apotheosis; it stopped abruptly half-way through the love episode. Jacoby said the scheme was faulty through absence of a male character. I threw these poems away some months ago, and don't regret having done so, as they had a most exciting effect on my nerves, without satisfying the critical instinct. I was in the middle of a rather scandalous novel about myself, a youth without a father and just a suspicion of illegitimacy to make him romantic, when real events awakened me rather startlingly.

The following lines, however, were found on a loose sheet of paper in an empty notebook:

London girls, London girls,
    how I admire you!
London girls, London girls,
    how I desire you!

London girls, London girls,
    do I inspire you?
    Homage to London girls always.

When the fresh blood of youth
    through my proud veins runs tingling,
I put on my coat and
    with crowds go mingling;
And one of them beckons,
    I smile at another,
And one is reproving and says she's a mother.
    London girls, etc.

O London, marvel of pavements and vi'lets,
And radiant sins by the lamplighted islets,
Where heaven descends upon labouring
    faces,
And joy goes the journey she never retraces!
    London girls, etc.

If death blots my youth out,
    and more is the pity,
Let him come in the arteried heart of the city,
And traffic roar over my prostrate adoring,
While cheeks are yet pink and the passions
    yet soaring.
    London girls, etc.

XXXII

I was sitting at the table writing about half past two, when the front-door bell rang; I often used to answer it to save the maid trouble. Judge my surprise to see Woodenleg, who handed me a telegram, which had been delivered that morning. "Come York Hotel immediately Arabella Bollond." So my aunt was staying with Father. I lost no time in putting on my shoes—I had not been out that morning, and thanking Woodenleg, walked, partly with him, to the hotel. I could not be bothered to take a bus, I suppose because I wanted exercise. There was some commotion when I gave the porter my name, and my aunt stopped me outside Father's door with, "Why have you been so long? Do you know your father is very seriously ill?"

"How should I?"

"No, you mustn't go in," for I was turning the door-handle. "Come downstairs."

We sat in an empty corner of the lounge, and she told me that my father had died of a stroke when getting up that morning. A postcard from her lay on the dressing-table conspicuously, so she was summoned from Richmond at once, and interviewed the doctor, who said nothing could have been done. She then routed out my Marchmont Street address from Father's papers, and sent off the telegram. She said I had cruelly neglected him, and, losing my temper, I left the hotel, bidding her let me know when and where the funeral would take place. She followed me to the door, but I paid no attention to her; my last words were spoken in the lounge. I walked back to Maida Vale in a towering rage and at a furious pace. I was still clenching my fists and ruffling my hair when Jacoby returned and I told him the news. He was at once extremely sympathetic, and I realized that I was now an orphan and deserving of pity on that account. I told him quite honestly that it was impossible for me to feel heartbroken at my bereavement, although I always respected my father. All his death meant was that I should now probably be on strained terms with my aunt for the rest of her days, and forced before long into some thoroughly uncongenial occupation like clerking in a drab office. He said I must for the present look on his mother's house as my home, and advised me that evening, if I could control myself sufficiently, to write a letter to my aunt regretting my passion, but saying that I was hurt at the suggestion of neglect, and offering to do all I could for her, entreating an early reply. That, he added, would save me the awkward business of going round again to the hotel, unless (I admired the frank way he said this) I was particularly desirous of seeing my father's corpse. I wrote the letter the next day; my own composition entirely—Jacoby never saw it at all—it ran thus:

"Dear Aunt Arabella, I am sorry to have forgotten myself so completely yesterday, but there are some suggestions one resents at any time; but I do not want to say any more about this. I am sorry and hope to be forgiven.

"What can I do now? Can I help in any way? I know you have done everything for Father that could be done. Ought I to stay at the hotel? Will you tell me what to do? Believe me, I am only anxious to be as little in the way as possible at this terrible time for you. When is the funeral?

"Your affectionate nephew,
"Reginald Bollond."

I kept saying to myself "When is the funeral?" at odd times of the day. Jacoby, who was kindness itself, told me to read poetry, and in the interval between the above letter and Aunt Arabella's reply I devoured, without properly understanding them, Ernest Dowson's poems and two books of Francis Thompson's, which I liked because of their won't-shut-up quality.

My aunt wrote in this style:

"Dear Reginald, I hope I shall never have to go through another day like yesterday. I believe you will find the burden of your father's death easier to bear than I. You can help by remaining where you are. The funeral is on Thursday. Will you be home on Wednesday evening in time for dinner? The Brooks have very kindly left the house at our disposal. The doctor and Major Sinclair are helping me about the railway journey. I enclose money for your ticket. Don't write to me again; I depend on your coming on Wednesday.

"Your affectionate aunt,

"Arabella."

I was indignant that, as the only son of my father now in England, I was not invited to take a larger part in the funeral arrangements, but consoled myself with the thought that a lot of pain and inconvenience was thus spared me.

XXXIII

There were nearly three days before I was expected home, and during them Jacoby made himself fully acquainted with my family history. He urged me to wear a black suit of his, which fitted me astonishingly well, if only for the funeral, and repeated that the scene at the hotel was a gross error on my part, and that I ought to do everything I could to efface its impression from my aunt's mind. I begged him to leave me alone and give me more poetry to read, so I sat reading in front of the fire, never leaving the house, in a dissatisfied mood, feeling that whatever I did in future would be wrong, and that it was quite useless to be agreeable; I should give myself away however I acted. The idea struck me that my father had been loyal to me when alive, but now his spirit was floating about telling everyone I knew or was likely to know, "My son Reginald is a blackguard; don't you have anything to do with him." The truth was that I had got myself into a morbid and highly imaginative state by reading so many books without proper preparation. At last, meaning to free myself from these fancies, I walked round to Roderick Ames' lodgings, assured that he would be the best cold douche possible. It was about half past six and he was out. As I came away from the door, a girl with a close-fitting bonnet walked up to it. "Are you wanting Mr. Ames?" I asked, "for, if so, he is out."

"Indeed I don't want Roderick Ames," she retorted, "I know too much about him. Are you a friend of his?"

"I have only met him once," I said.

"Then you are lucky," she replied. "I shouldn't advise you to see too much of him"; and she rang the bell. I was moving on.

"Don't go," she said, "I am only leaving a note." The woman came to the door rather in a huff, thinking that I had rung again, but changed her tone when the girl handed her a note for Miss Coe and said there was no answer. When the door was closed, she turned to me, "Are you going anywhere in particular?"

"No," I said, "but I wish you would talk to me; I have just lost my father."

"I am going to talk to you about Roderick Ames," she said, ignoring my plea. "He's not a person for any young man to know—he's a degenerate."

"I confess," I said in a worldly manner, "I found him a pleasant enough companion. Everyone's a little odd, don't you think?"

"Perhaps," she said quite coldly, "you want to find yourself in the hands of the police; that would be a new experience for you."

"It would indeed," I replied. "What is your name?"

"Damn you!" she broke out.

"I like you," I said; "you meant well warning me. You needn't tell me your name unless you like; mine's Roy Bollond."

She gave me a look that cut me to the quick; it was like an honest child punished for something it hadn't done. "Dorothy Earle," she said. "I'm your sister." I find it hard to explain what went through me on hearing this. I knew it was all filthy sentimentalism, that she was no more my sister than the Queen was, that if she were a *demi-mondaine* down on her luck she might just as well have said so; but although these thoughts certainly passed through my head at the time, I felt, absurd as it may sound, that I had come to the end of the world, and that there was an enormous stretch of ocean encircling me and the figure of this girl at my side.

Literally everything was wiped out, I was unconscious of the street, of her appearance even. I must have looked abnormal, for in quite a different tone she exclaimed,

"Whatever's the matter? You're not starving, are you?"

"It's all right," I said; "I won't go and see Ames again. Will you tell me where you live?"

She pulled out a grubby card from her reticule, and said, "I am generally in about half past four."

"I shall come and see you," I said with decision, and walked home.

Reading through this account of my first meeting with Dorothy, I confess that I must have left something out, but what I cannot think; I have shown it to her, and she says it is verbally accurate. All the same I cannot believe that two strangers ever met in such an outlandish way; more must have been said, there were finer shades, no doubt. Would any other woman have spoken as she spoke of Ames except to a personal friend?

Dorothy says she is exceptional; perhaps so. But the more I think of it, the more unreal this episode appears.

XXXIV

Jacoby asked if anything fresh was the matter. I said I had had an adventure with a girl. He sneered. "Girls are the ruin of everyone. A man starts out to write poetry, merely for the sake of doing it. So long as he does that he is all right. Then comes the idea of ambition; he thinks he can't be a real poet unless he writes to and about a girl—that's what will happen to you. The girl doesn't care twopence for what he does, she just wants him, so much flesh and blood, and she gets him, and he's finished. Dowson, whom you were reading yesterday, was like that."

"You're a fool," I said hotly (he liked me to get my rag out, as he called it, or arguing from yourself, which is just as bad). "I don't want to be literary or write, it's you that are forcing me into the groove. I just want to wander about, or sit in front of a fire, liked by everyone, and damn it all, I'm going to get it, character or no character."

"Whatever are you talking about?" he shouted, walking up and down. "Who mentioned character?"

"Well, girls or no girls, if you like that better," I growled, stretching out my legs, and, as I did so, a funny thought struck me. "I wish I'd been born in a stable," I said audibly.

"You mean," he said, shoving his head forward, "that you'd like to wear riding-breeches and leggings, and lean against walls and doors, sucking a straw."

"God!" I roared. "However did you guess that?"

"Do you think I can't see through you? You're as transparent as glass."

"Well, if you know all that, tell me why I want to wear that costume."

"Because you are half educated and love mud; it's easier to get. Beauty's beyond you, you know that; so you say to yourself, 'Suppose I become a filthy little beast, and pander to everybody's worst side, how nice that would be.' Why, you've got no ideals at all."

"I don't know so much about that," I said, looking very wise (I saw my face in the mirror opposite), and thinking of Lucy: "But suppose you are right, and I have none; I can't get them, can I?"

"No, you can't," he said, "but you might have some notion of duty."

"Duty," I said, "is to get as much fun out of life as possible, giving as little trouble to others as possible in the process."

"Why not as much trouble, for that matter?"

"Because there's such a thing as compensation, and your wrongdoings generally recoil on you in the long run, and I for my part ain't going to take any risks."

"You took a risk with your aunt."

"I lost my temper, you mean."

"The stable-boy ideal," he went on, ignoring me and looking at the fire—"we'll call it that, if you don't mind, is all very well if you've got money and with it the knowledge that all the time you are something quite different from what you seem. A person really of that class wants to look a gentleman, and the most degraded characters wear patent boots and spats. You wouldn't do that, would you?"

"I would do anything," I replied with conviction.

"I'll remember that," he said, eyeing me with contempt.

He then went on to speak of a man he had known when he first came to London, who deliberately made his life an ugly thing; he would not go into details, but he gave me to understand that there was no hope for him. The question was, was he happy? His desires were satisfied; of course, as he got older, the things he wanted would be harder to get, but he could always say he had them once; but what was left now, except boredom?

That was the punishment of evildoers; he could not imagine a worse.

"One need never be bored," I said, "unless one is condemned always to remain in one place, and then possibly one begins to notice little things that escaped one before, like Bruce and the spider. That's the advantage of getting into prison, no doubt."

"You are sensible," he said, "to have thought about prison, though the chances are against your ending up in one; you are not conceited or vindictive enough for that."

"Tell me," I cried, happy for the first time that day, "have you known anyone who got into prison, and if so, did it spoil them?"

"I knew one man," he said, "who got in for a false reference, an odd case with a mixture of chivalry in it; he was befriending a woman out of work; a woman again, you see, getting a man into trouble. He looked rather smarter when he came out, and exceptionally pleased with himself."

"I should certainly be that," I said, "if I got second division."

"But you wouldn't," he laughed.

"Well, there's no knowing, is there? And did your friend look starved?"

"No, I can't say that."

"Have you heard of anyone called Ames in London—Roderick Ames?"

"Can't say I have. What of him?"

"Nothing in particular; I thought he was notorious."

"I don't know notorious people."

"But you might have heard of him, and I'm now satisfied that he isn't notorious, as I was told."

"I don't make a study of criminals," he said, "though I should like to hear your accounts of them from time to time. And now let us have something to eat."

XXXV

It was after dinner that the event occurred which made me what I am. I was going to my old home next day, and said I felt I should not come back again, that some dreadful provision had been made for me by my father's will, by which I was bound not to come to London more than once a year. I had heard of a son inheriting a fortune on condition that he never went within eighty miles of Piccadilly, and I suppose this made me apprehensive. Jacoby in a startling manner exclaimed, "Look here, Bollond! I love you. You are necessary to me. Consider that you always have a home where I am, do you hear?" There was almost severity in his tone, and I was just able to suppress the words that leapt up in me, "Very well; if you want me to live on you, you fool, I will." Instead, I pretended to be overcome, hid my face in my hands, and went to bed almost immediately. Upstairs, after undressing, I ran about the room like a ballet dancer. "You've got him, you little devil," I cried, "you've got him, without ever really trying for him. Now you have to keep him, quite another matter."

When I was half asleep, he came in without knocking and sat down at the foot of the bed.

"What is it?" I muttered.

"I want to be with you," he said; "I am sure you are lonely."

"Don't be like a woman. I'm quite all right, thank you, till after the funeral."

"You don't know how fond I am of you."

"Show it now by going away."

"Do you really want me to go?"

"Of course I do. I can't love you because I already love a woman. It's best to be honest. Good night."

He made a kind of moan and went away.

No reference to the incident was made by either of us at breakfast, though it was pretty clear that he had not slept a wink. He went to work as usual, and I wandered round the house, as if it were mine, until lunch. I wanted to know why he disliked women, and thought I might come upon some reason by an examination of his books. I soon found two printed volumes of poems, which on inspection proved to be by his mother; they were wishy-washy, and, like most second-rate verse, about unsatisfied yearnings, and nothing else. Out of one of them dropped a letter, to "Julia", which I took the liberty of reading. It was a most effusive pathetic affair, whether written by or to Mrs. Jacoby I could not tell, though the latter supposition seemed more probable, as it referred to a certain boy, evidently the recipient's son: "He only needs you," it said, "he will never need another," and it exhorted Julia to keep the boy entirely to herself, to make a world of two people, over whom the writer apparently would sit as a presiding angel. The conclusion I drew, hazardous, on the evidence, I admit, was that Jacoby's mother had carefully brought him up to believe in nobody but her, and still exercised a strong hold on him, where other women were concerned. I have since found that this habit is common with mothers of only sons, and accounts for aberrations in the boys when they are about sixteen. In fact a mother's love is a dangerous thing, and can play all manner of pranks, unless the son is keen-witted enough to see through it, and even if he is, custom may pull him back.

In the case of Jacoby I have already explained that he was sceptical as regards his mother, and openly ridiculed her; but I was later to realize how completely she still dominated him without his knowledge.

However, my reflections on this matter were cut short for the present by the necessity of catching my train after lunch and the gloomy frame of mind suggested by my home-coming and the sight of my aunt.

XXXVI

The Brooks had taken over our country place lock, stock and barrel. I fancy I may have said this before, but cannot bother to look back and see. On the suggestion of the rector, who always loved my father, they had moved into the rectory for a day and a half, so that the house might be to all intent and purpose ours during the funeral, and they had instructed their staff to wait on us. Kindness always upsets me, and I very nearly broke down when their chauffeur met me coming out of the station, so that when I stood face to face with my aunt in the drawing-room, I looked the picture of a penitent boy, and was forgiven at once. What's more, the black suit found favour, and I mentioned Jacoby's mother—he had advised me to do this—and my aunt was visibly relieved to think I was the guest of really nice people in London.

Major Sinclair, whom I remembered visiting us when I was small, also treated me kindly, and did not put me in awe of him. Dinner was a quiet meal; we talked mainly of how things would be after the war, and the major made us smile by saying that prices had been too low before it, and there was no just cause for complaint now. Afterwards we regretted my father's lonely existence in the country and his pride in standing aloof, because he knew he was unable to keep up the estate; the result was that, although the oldest family in those parts, we were looked upon as utter strangers by everyone except the rectory and Lady Maltear; the hearse apart, her carriage was the only conveyance at the funeral. I slept in my old room, thanks to my aunt, and dreamt of Lucy, who told me that she hated Mr. Castle, but with my permission was going to marry him; I don't remember if I gave it.

The morning was a typical drizzly December day. The funeral was timed for noon, and we waited for the Leicester lawyer, who had my father's will. He came at eleven, and I avoided him, as I did not want to give the impression that I wanted money. My aunt nearly collapsed at the graveside and I got giddy gazing down at the coffin. The rector looked kindly at me, I thought, and I wondered if I might even cadge a week at the rectory on the strength of his friendship with my father.

Afterwards rough refreshment was served in the dining-room, and we sat round listening to the will. Imagine my surprise to learn that when I was twenty-one I should be entitled to two hundred pounds a year beyond what my mother had left me. Until that time my aunt was my guardian, and money would be paid her for my benefit. I did not pretend to be overcome by the news, and Major Sinclair said he believed I would prove in every way worthy of my father. My aunt desired to speak to me alone before I left. The major and the lawyer went away together.

XXXVII

"And now, Reggie," she said, "you have heard how you are placed, not well off for these times. What are you going to make of your life?"

"You will be annoyed at what I shall say," I answered, "so I would rather ask you what allowance you intend to make me until I come of age."

"You cannot annoy me now," she said, and there was conviction in her tone. "I will answer your question when you have answered mine."

"Well," I said, "you will say this is no answer, but I intend that life should make me. The chances of getting on the stage, or making a living when one is on, are a hundred to one against; I haven't the cheek to say that I am going to be a writer, though I feel, who doesn't at my age, that I have a novel in me—" and I paused for effect.

"For heaven's sake—" she exclaimed in real anguish, "don't be an idler."

"Don't worry about me," I said, "but let me know how I am placed."

"I am going to allow you two pounds a week," she said, "which I will send you regularly, eight pounds on the first of the month, as you are not old enough to have a banking account; so you must let me know your changes of address. It was your father's wish, for we often discussed you in London that I should keep in touch with you, and I hope you will come out to Rickmansworth for a week-end now and again, and certainly spend Christmas with me, unless you are unavoidably detained elsewhere. I expect you on the 22nd coming. Be a good boy, Reggie." And she turned her head away. I had not the heart to ask her for two pounds on the spot, but she gave it me before I left.

When I was in the car I remembered that I had not enquired after Molly and Hal. That looked heartless.

XXXVIII

Once in the train, I exclaimed that my aunt
was a hopeless fool. Fancy sending cash by the
month! Unless I had a miser's spirit, that eight
pounds would go in ten days. A little reflec-
tion showed me that keeping off the money
tack when I came to town had deluded my
father into supposing that I was a thrifty
youth and could be trusted with lump sums
instead of small doles, and that was the reason
for this rash experiment, I had now sufficient
knowledge of the world to be sure that, until
one was known to have come into money, one
was much happier living poorly and on charity; besides, one learned so much more that
way; so I decided on no account to tell Jacoby,
or indeed anyone, that I had more than five
pounds a month, if that, from all sources.
To this plan I strictly adhered, and gained a
great deal of pleasure from it, for on occasions

when I was bored, I would pay two or three pounds for a seat at boxing matches, which I greatly enjoyed, and told nobody where I had been. Thus I did not hoard my money, though I kept two pounds in an inner pocket against emergencies (made a practice of this), but had its full joy.

When I got back, I put on a sad face, and cleared the ground by asking Jacoby if he would mind listening to my financial position. He was flattered at this mark of friendship, and I told him that until I was of age, when I should inherit £120 a year, all told, I was entirely at the mercy of my aunt, who refused to say how much she would allow me, but had started off with two pounds (what a relief to tell the truth once!); she said she would send me money by the week—this was a safe statement, as I knew she would write once a week—but she was a thrifty woman and dreadfully obstinate; I was expected to stay with her over Christmas.

Jacoby was thoroughly pleased with my diplomacy, whether or not he suspected my lies, for in this regard he was inscrutable, and, without looking for evil, did not like people any better for being good. He had put me into another room, as he was entertaining his mother for a week, and she was arriving next day. He said he did not feel justified in asking me to take her off his hands in the first days of my bereavement, but I said I was only too glad to have something to do, and hinted judiciously that my father would have been the last to wish me to martyrize myself on his account, and that I remembered him saying (invention, of course) that he went to the theatre a week after his mother died. As a result I was deputed to meet Mrs. Jacoby at Victoria, as he would be at work until the usual hour; and his description of her was so circumstantial that I recognized her on the platform with no difficulty.

Mrs. Jacoby was a woman whom the world had treated well in this respect, that her age became her, and she took no pains to conceal it; for this cause she was regarded as a lady of distinction by all who met her, and, as she had little or no feminine jealousy, her cranks made her even lovable.

She was without a maid, at which I pretended to be surprised, using her self-sufficiency as the occasion of an early compliment.

"So you are Arthur's new friend," she said. "You are younger than I thought. You must tell me about him; I am sure he is unhappy in his work, for he never tells me what he does. Have you told the man where to drive?

Do you think my case is safe in front? No, I always have my dressing-bag inside with me."

"Mrs. Jacoby," I said, defining my strategy at once by a sure instinct, "I am very anxious indeed about Arthur, for a reason I would rather not tell you, and am really glad you have given me the chance of being open with you."

"Tell me everything," she said, taking to me, as I knew she would. Emboldened, I began.

XXXIX

What does it matter what I said? I hardly remember, except that it was admirably adapted to that sort of woman. Affection for her son, who had been so good to me, then a check, as if kindness wasn't a thing over which to sentimentalize, then fears that he was too much wrapped up in himself; if only a woman were in the house! No, his work did not suit him; but wasn't it lucky to get work at all in these days? Her voice said as clear as type, "This is a sensible boy, and perhaps has a good influence on Arthur."

Just before we stopped at the house, I whispered, "Don't please, let Arthur know I have discussed him with you; I have really no right to discuss anyone, at a loose end, as I am."

"It will suit us," I saw her register mentally, "to keep him at a loose end." I insisted on paying the man.

XL

I was not present at the meeting of mother and son, but judged that it could not have been very affectionate from what was said at dinner. Jacoby apologized for the state of the house, about which his mother had grumbled all lunch. I must confess I did not see much amiss, but I had little experience of the insides of houses, and country servants are notoriously untidy.

"I am ashamed," she said, "that you should have asked a friend into such a pigsty. Why did you not tell me that Mabel was leaving to get married? We must have another maid while I am here, and I feel half inclined to give this one notice."

"I shouldn't do that, Mother," he said, appealing to me with a nervous twinkle, but it was not my game to save the situation.

"Why shouldn't I?" she exclaimed; "I never have any difficulty with servants." (I believed her, as she always lived in hotels.) "While I am here, this house must be run on my lines. What do you say to that?" turning to me, "I did not catch your name?"

"Reggie; I'd rather *you* called me that than 'Mr. Bollond'." Jacoby flushed, as I had meant him to do, for I had never said such a thing to him.

"I don't like shortened names," she said abruptly, "and I suppose no one calls you Reginald?"

"Call him Reggie and have done with it," growled Jacoby.

So they both called me Reggie henceforward.

Afterwards the china cat was unpacked and placed in the centre of the drawing-room mantelpiece, and we rearranged the furniture till bedtime. Jacoby was too sulky to speak more than a dozen words to me. I was assiduous in helping his mother, and, when she learned that we once had a country place, I saw that my footing in that house was better assured.

XLI

It is perhaps odd that I had no girl friends.
Who knows? If I had, my life might have
worked out quite differently. By girl friends I
mean a number of aimless girls, to whom one
can go when one is bored, and who, without
demanding anything more than the price of
a meal (which often enough they are ready to
pay), are quite contented for the young fellow
to be hanging round, not greatly smitten with
anyone in particular. I think the reason was
that in my early schooldays I had considerable experience of girls, and got into trouble
on their account. There was one who lived
with her mother and cousin a minute or two
beyond bounds, on whom I paid secret visits,
until one of the prefects caught me, and let me
off a beating, provided he was introduced. In
the end I was beaten as well, for the wicked
creature invited us both in separate letters at

the same hour a week later. And then there was another (this first I met out on a run, when I was limping with a sprain; she gave me a lift in the car she was driving, joy-rides were strictly forbidden), in a sweet shop, who presented me with a lock of her auburn hair without my asking; of course I made it up to her with a sash or something of the sort. The fact is I realized quite early that I was attractive to girls, and, knowing I could obtain their favours easily, fought shy of them, as one does in one's youth with things that are at one's feet.

The trouble with me has always been that I am attractive. I speak entirely without vanity, in the obvious meaning of the word; I draw people to me, they like to catch hold of my arm and put their mouths close to mine when speaking physical charm, I suppose, yet heaps of far better-looking men than I have no such power. I was almost frigid to Jacoby's mother for the first five minutes, and though I would not pretend for a moment that she was in the least in love with me, I found her thumb on my wrist; so it can have nothing to do with a desire to make myself agreeable. The two people with whom my life has been most closely bound up own to this quality in me, but say that it has had no effect on their feelings for me one way or another, though they certainly did not object to it. I remember a boy, who sat next to me in form my second term, saying he wanted to hit me. I asked him why. He said there were people you wanted to hit, just because they were round. I don't think I was rounder than most people he knew, or aggressively cheerful for that matter. No, it's a case of attractiveness, that's all.

Now attractiveness has its dangers, and if there is any moral in what I am writing, and there must be, because there is a moral or purpose in everything one does, though one may not be conscious of it at the time, it is that an attractive person is greatly to be pitied, for he does himself a good deal of harm by simply being what he is. No one has accused me of malice or threats, but it has been said to my face that I lead people on and land them in tight corners, which is an accusation levelled against women, with justice perhaps; but no man likes to be called a tempter and that word has actually been used of me. On the contrary, whenever I have given way to temptation, it has been because I took the line of least resistance under the circumstances in consideration for the other person's feelings. But who will believe that, I should like to know, where money is concerned?

XLII

As yet I had told Mrs. Jacoby nothing of my family affairs, but at eleven the next morning (she breakfasted in bed), finding me lying on the library hearth-rug with some book or other, she sympathetically told me not to move, and asked if there was anything that would give me pleasure. I said I thought not, but should like to feel that I was of use.

"My dear boy," she said, sitting down quite naturally beside me with the grace of a younger woman, and warming her long fingers; how the diamond ring shone in the fire glow! "Arthur has told me of your trouble. I think you are so brave."

"It is an awful bore, Father dying," I said, "as we were just beginning to understand each other's point of view."

"You must not speak of him as dead," she said in a shocked voice; "he has passed over, and now you will be able to understand each other better."

I looked at her in surprise.

"Ah!" she said in a knowing tone, "you are sceptical; a great joy awaits you."

"The deuce it does!" I thought, and continued to stare.

"Don't be frightened, Reggie," she said, stroking me; "we will see in a day or two, that is, if you are quite willing, if we can get *en rapport* with him."

"No, thank you," I said, shaking myself free and quite forgetting manners; "I hate spiritualism and all that sort of thing. Besides, when people are dead, you should leave them in peace."

"Poor boy," she whispered, "poor, poor boy."

"That is indeed true, Mrs. Jacoby," I said, "as I haven't a penny of my own before I am of age."

"What does money matter?" she exclaimed, with the genuine astonishment of one who has had it all her life. I could say nothing, for I was pondering how far I should humour her in her desire to meet my dead father, and, never having been faced with such a difficulty, and loathing superstitions like snakes, was completely nonplussed.

"It is true," I heard her say to herself, "that he is very young, but Sophy's child was fifteen," and then aloud, "Has anyone told you that you would make a good medium?"

"It was my father's dying wish," I said with great difficulty, which she took for emotion (really I was staggered by the monstrosity of her assertion), "that I should never, never meddle with anything occult"—I pronounced the word as if it meant obscene—"and that is true!" I eyed her for a moment, and burst into a splutter, the nearest approach to hysterics I could manage, hiding my face in the hearth-rug. She was all over me in two minutes. I did the "brave man surprised into emotion" stunt for what I was worth. "Mrs. Jacoby," I said, "you have taken me off my guard. I know you believe in these things, but I don't; I'd rather not."

She patted me. "Now you don't see anything wrong," she said coaxingly, "in my looking into a crystal, do you? I have such a pretty one upstairs."

And she went out of the room to fetch it. Down went my head in my hands. Should I be consistent or not? I tossed up a penny; heads give in, tails stand out. Tails had it. I was adamant when she returned. "Excuse me," I

140

said in my politest voice, "but I am going for a short walk; can I get you anything?" She saw the game was up, and gave me a shilling to buy some sealing-wax. I went out, leaving her with the crystal.

XLIII

I knew of course that I should pay for this; one always pays where a woman is in the business but I could not blame myself, although I had deliberately frustrated my interests. Why! she might have made a Yogi of me. Bobby Chiffham, whom I met not long afterwards at Ames', told me he knew a fellow, not unlike me to look at, but swarthier, who practised ascetic meditation in a delightful little flat off Gloucester Road, which had been found for him and furnished by a woman. Bobby said he didn't believe in the rubbish any more than I did, but he saw she took an interest in him and feathered his nest accordingly.

Still, you can't run counter to instinct; it is the same in everything. I certainly have a filthier mind than most people, but I can't wrap my filthiness up in fine long words and pretend it is beautiful; so I am unable to see eye to eye with certain acquaintances, just as filthy-minded; they say I am coarse. I don't excuse myself, they do. But I am rambling. Mrs. Jacoby told her son that I was highly neurotic, and that the proper place for me was a nursing-home. She said I shrieked aloud when she brought down the crystal, and people passing the house stopped and stared in. The noise I made was, as I may have said, a spluttering noise and a gulp, which could hardly be heard in the passage, also it was over before she went out for the crystal. I don't know to this day which of us Jacoby believed, me probably, as he had no sympathy with his mother's hobbies. I admired him for not taking sides.

XLIV

She prolonged her stay by three days, into which a great deal was concentrated; before these only two events happened worth mentioning. Jacoby told me he had an incurable but not an infectious complaint, and could not live for more than three years; would I sleep with him? I asked for a day to think it over. In great agony of mind I called on Dorothy Earle. She was out, so I left a note saying that I wanted her help, and would call the following afternoon. I did not mean to mention that matter to her, I only wanted to feel that there was a woman near me who had my welfare at stake. I went on to Lucy, who lived the other side of London; she was not at home. I was frightened that Mrs. Jacoby might suspect me of seducing her son, and was now alternately attracted and repelled by her. I seemed to be absolutely without a guide. I was so sorry for

Jacoby, fearing that the wait till the following evening would be more painful to him than to me. I solved the problem of that evening by going to a music-hall, which he thought sinful and heartless of me. I cried when I went to sleep, and, though I am not in the least religious, got out of bed to pray for him, laughing at myself, when I awoke, for having done so. Next morning I went to the British Museum, and stood quite ten minutes before the Apollo in the Aeginetan room: I knew I should do the right thing now. Mrs. Jacoby was out to lunch with friends in Kensington; a relief for me. I slept for an hour afterwards, and then walked round to Dorothy, hardly a quarter of an hour away, near the canal.

"I thought you would come earlier," she said; "but what's the trouble?"

She had a little room on the second floor of the house, of which the plaster outside and wallpaper inside were peeling off in dirty strips. She sat on her bed, which was clean, and I on a chair, facing her, in front of an empty grate.

"My father is dead," I said, "and I feel rudderless."

"Would it help you," she said in a cold dead practical voice, "to hear the miseries of a whore?"

I asked if she were still one. She said one must always be consistent and true to type, if one was to get anything at all out of life.

"And what am I then?"

"Oh, you're a joy-boy."

"What's that?"

"Don't fish for compliments."

"Is it a nice thing?"

"I should think very nice."

In five minutes she convinced me that there was nothing to make me miserable, and that life, if you trusted it, was a fine thing for everyone, rich and poor. I asked her repeatedly if I could be of any use to her; she said none whatever, but that we clearly were agreeable to each other, and I ought to put all thought of help and use out of my mind in our relations. She refused to call on me at Jacoby's, but said she would write. She kissed me affectionately at parting.

When he came back from work, I told Jacoby that I would come to his room at half past ten that night, but would rather wait till his mother went away. He said he understood what I felt, but no harm would come to me; he did not say that his mother understood, and I did not ask him. I kept my word, as he could not wait even a day in suspense. I now come to the last three days of her stay, Saturday, Sunday, Monday; she left on Tuesday morning.

XLV

After breakfast on Saturday Father Morris was announced. He was a tall thin man, rather blue about the cheeks. I said Mrs. Jacoby would be down presently.

"Is Arthur in?" he asked.

"Arthur is at work," I said. "He will be sorry to have missed you, for he has often mentioned your name."

"I am glad to hear that," he said in a husky voice, "as I have not seen him for a great number of years, and he is not a Catholic."

"I am sure there is something in Roman Catholicism," I said; "you are all so sure of yourselves. There was a boy at school who could stand any amount of ragging, I never understood why, till he told me that he was so sure of his protecting saint that nothing else mattered."

Father Morris seemed a little put out by this naive panegyric, and said after a pause that there were a good many people on the threshold of the Church without knowing it; and sometimes they remained there all their lives.

"Would you say," I asked, "that I am a Catholic type?"

"I do not know you," he answered shortly.

"That is a pity," I went on, "for I feel that I might be of great use persuading people. I am very persuasive, though I do not mean to be so. Now if I had it from you that I was a Catholic, or going that way, I should really be eased in mind," (I liked talking to this man) "for I hate the thought of wasted opportunities. You wouldn't call me conceited, would you? But I do think I was put into the world for some useful purpose, but so far I have not quite succeeded in finding out what it is."

"You are a friend of Arthur Jacoby?" he asked.

"Yes, and troubled about him; he is not at all happy"—but at that moment the door opened, admitting Mrs. Jacoby, who gracefully ordered me out of the room.

I was wondering where to go, as the maids were making my bed, when the front-door bell rang. I let in a young man in khaki. "Is Arthur in?" he asked.

"No, but his mother is."

"And who are you?"

"Bollond, a friend of his."

"Look here," he said, "my name's Cameron, Hugh Cameron. How is Arthur?"

I could not make up my mind what to say, because his face attracted me, it was so clean and frank. I could not look him straight in the eyes; I felt I ought not to be seen talking to him. Only once at school have I had this feeling for anyone. It passed, however.

"Arthur is queer, very queer," I said heedlessly, "and what is worse, affectionate."

Cameron laughed, but did not take his eyes off me. "You know of course that he's not a sane man like you or me."

"Why do you come to see him, then?"

"Because I'm his cousin, on the father's side. I was brought up with him. Has he work now? He had a comparatively easy time in the Army?"

"Oh yes, he has Government work all right, but he wants company. He makes me read all kinds of outlandish books on art. I'm no use to him, not nearly strong-willed enough."

"I can't wait now," he said, "and I don't want to see his mother. This is my address. I'm here in the holidays" (handing me a card).

"Tell Arthur I will look in on Tuesday on the chance of seeing him, at——"

"Six," I suggested; "he will be back by then, and Mrs. Jacoby will have left."

"Don't forget—Cameron." And he went away, smiling at me. Forgetting that Father Morris had not yet gone, I walked into the dining-room. "Here he comes," said Mrs. Jacoby. "No, don't go away again. Father Morris and I think that Arthur is in a critical state and you excite him."

"I assure you," I said, "that I can't help it. He asked me to stay here. I do what I can for him."

"I am suggesting," she said gently, "that both you and he want a change. I have told Father Morris of your bereavement, and we are glad to think you are spending Christmas with relations."

"Has Arthur said anything to you about me?" I asked Mrs. Jacoby.

"Only that he is fond of you and does not want another brother."

"Then you think it is good for him that I should go? Have you mentioned *that* to him?"

"Not yet."

"If I go now, I have nowhere to stay." How I hated these people!

"We do not want to *turn you out,*" said Father Morris, looking at me gravely.

"I suppose," I blurted out, losing control, "that you want to get hold of Arthur before he dies, make a Catholic of him, and secure his money."

"Who told you," said Mrs. Jacoby in a sepulchral tone, "that he *had* money?"

The priest was unmoved.

"Who told me?" I said hysterically. "I don't know really; but I'm one of those people who know without being told. I wish you good luck; I'm going."

And out I went; I was not going to stop another half-hour in that house. It took me ten minutes to put my things together and make a note of what was at the wash. This note I slipped into a letter to Jacoby, which ran thus, as far as I can remember:

"Dear Jacoby, Your mother and the priest suggest (your mother quite nicely) that I am a bad influence, and the sooner you and I are separated the better. So I am leaving at once. I will call on Monday, when the washing comes back, for the things mentioned in the enclosed list. I have not been the friend to you perhaps that I might, but have done what I could the short time we have been together. Thank you once and for all for your kindness.

     "Yours" (I hesitated here)
       "affectionately,
       "R. Bollond."

 "An officer called Cameron came to see you this morning and is coming on Tuesday at six."

Jacoby was reading *Mademoiselle de Maupin*, and had the book by his bedside. I put the letter against the leaf that was turned down and shut up the book. His mother and Father Morris were still talking when I left the house, but did not hear me go. What was my next move?

XLVI

The heaviness of the suitcase, which, as I have explained, was half full of bottles, made me go no farther than I could help. I went to Dorothy, who met me outside her front door.

"Can you put me up?" I said; "I'll pay."

"Of course you'll pay," she said. "Anyone could see that about you; and I'll put you up. But why have you come so suddenly?"

I told her the situation in a few words.

"Quite right," she said emphatically, "quite, quite right! I hardly thought you would have the pluck. Of course they are after his money; he must have it in his own right. There will be a scene between mother and son now you have left the house. Whose is it, by the way?"

"The house? Mrs. Jacoby's, I believe."

"You'll hear all about it when you call on Monday; someone will be bound to nail you."

"You have a vivid imagination."

"Have I? Well, perhaps I have. Take that case up to my room. I'll be back in twenty minutes or thereabouts."

I did as she told me, and she was up to time, returning with eatables, which we spread on the bed. "I hope you don't mind sharing a room with me," she said; "for one thing, there isn't another spare room in the house; for another, I want to sleep in the same bed as you, to have you curled, like a little furry animal, at my side. You do blush nicely, you immoral boy."

"Who owns the house?" said I. "Perhaps they might object to what you propose." .

She was greatly amused. "Why, old Daisy Perkins, and she'd love to see it filled with young men like you, only rich ones. I'm not after your money, now; don't get that into your head. I like your boots, Bollond; do you always wear patents?"

I had on a pair that Jacoby had given me. "Surely," I said, "it is the height of depravity to like people's boots."

"I don't eat them," she said, to my amazement. "I'll do them up for you in the morning with my fingers, not a button-hook."

"Don't get excited," I said. "I am extremely sorry if I fascinate you, I mean, if my boots do. I only want to be useful, and seriously, I am very much put out by what had just happened; I believe I should have grown really fond of Jacoby in a few months."

"Young men's sentimentalities disgust me besides being a sheer waste of time."

"Possibly you are right, but what about young girls' sentimentalities? In your life you must have indulged in some. There must be a girl for whom you would do almost anything, if she asked you."

"Yes," she said, "there is. Would you like to hear about her?"

"I'm not particularly anxious," I said, "unless you insist. Besides, the joy of these friendships disappears when you tell a third person."

"You're right there, and now will you sleep with me a little while, when these things are cleared away? I am very, very tired; I was awake all night with a racking headache. Don't take off your clothes, you lovely thing."

When the bed was straight, she lay down on it, and made me lie with my back towards her. She caught firmly hold of my waist with both hands, and rubbed her head against my back, between the shoulder blades, and kissed the nape of my neck; Mr. Castle's fur coat covered us. I couldn't sleep, and lay in that position, my mind a perfect blank, till close on five p.m.

XLVII

By that time I had a great desire to see a man. I am like that. When I am with a woman, I yearn for a man's company and his sharp direct common sense. When I am with men, I say to myself, "Oh, you are bores, all of you, deadly creatures of fact. Give me a woman any day." For a woman is light and airy, and charms you with her colour (men's dress is so drab) and movement; even if she is old, you are left with the movement: watch the play of an old woman's hand, and you will see what I mean. This is only the instinct for variety, planted in everybody, but with me it is acute, and I am really unhappy unless I am switched off, I can't think of a better word, from sex to sex pretty constantly. I knew if I went to Mr. Castle's flat, I should meet Lucy, and I was in no mood for ideals; at Marchmont Street was Woodenleg, who, when he did not talk literature, bully-ragged me for idleness; the one person left was Ames, and, going to him directly from Dorothy, when I had promised her never to see him again, appealed to me extremely just then. It is easy enough to say now that I ought never to have gone, and that my present plight is entirely due to my weakness in breaking my word; that is unfortunately true, but nothing could have kept me away from Ames that day, no, not a dozen Lucys.

I told Dorothy, when she woke, that I simply must have exercise, and agreed to meet her for dinner at a Soho restaurant, I forget which, at eight. I kept the appointment, but a great deal happened in those three hours. I wonder how shortly I can get it down, perhaps in two pages. I have made a study of reducing conversations to their lowest terms so far. Shall I leave this one out altogether? I think not. As far as words went, it was quite harmless certainly.

I walked to Shepherd's Market, and Ames himself opened the door, in smart togs. "Oh, it's you," he said, eyeing me as if I were a groom; "upstairs with you. I've got some people here, but wait till they are gone."

Any other day I should have resented this peremtory tone, but at the moment I positively revelled in it. I went upstairs, remembering to walk as he had taught me. The bedroom was tidier, but thick with smoke. I could distinguish three men sitting on chairs round a table, about to start a game of cards, I thought, but I was wrong, they had just finished. I heard one whisper to his neighbour, "Roddy's latest", as I came in.

"Stretch yourself on the bed, Bollond," said Ames, I suppose by way of introducing me to the company; "there's no room for another chair."

"Is he all right?" asked the man nearest me, Bobby Chiffham he was.

"Of course he is," said Ames, without looking at me. (I sat on the bed, having had enough of lying for one afternoon.) "Have you ever met anyone here who wasn't?"

"What about that French fellow, Raymond Bloc?"

"You mean," said a man with a creamy complexion and white eyebrows, "the fellow who stayed with Stokes and went off with his gold cigarette case."

"You have me there," said Ames, "but it was Hughie Stokes himself who told me he was all right." Everyone laughed.

"You undertake to get it," said the third man.

"Oh, yes," said Ames, "but you pay me in a week; no, I'll make it ten days."

I pricked up my ears; Ames was clearly a man to approach if one were in a tight corner.

"You'll be paid all right," said the white-haired man; "but how do you manage it? You've never failed a friend yet."

"That," said Ames, "is simply owing to luck."

"I must have the box by, Tuesday," said the third man, "else Jack will go clean off his chump. I'll come here for it about this time. Cheerio, all of you."

And he went out.

"What's all this about a box?" I enquired lazily from the bed; "is it set with precious stones, and why is Jack, whoever he is, in such a hurry for it?"

"Shall we tell him?" asked Bobby Chiffham.

"Tell him? Of course tell him," snorted the man with white eyebrows; "if you don't, he'll get it into his head that we are planning a burglary or something of the kind. My dear innocent," he went on, addressing me directly, "the box contains dope—yes, dope—cocaine. Now do you understand?"

"Oh, is that all?" I said wearily, ignoring him and looking at Ames. "It must be rather difficult to get now."

"Difficult!" exclaimed Ames with a note of pride. "I should just think it is. Why, I am the only man in London who knows where to get it."

I almost collapsed with laughter at the thought of this unique claim to distinction. After many years' attempts to shine in various unenviable lights, Ames could at last say that he was the only man in London who knew where to get cocaine. Under the struggle not to break down my face must have become serious, for he went on, "You see the importance of that."

"Indeed, I do," I said, "but it doesn't affect me personally, as I hate drugs and such messes."

"Is he really one of us?" asked Chiffham, and Ames replied with a villainously knowing grin, which the two men interpreted as a signal for their departure. They hardly noticed me, as he went out with them. I take back the sentence about the grin, it was knowing, but not villainous—but what does that matter?

"Well," he said, returning and locking the door, "what did you come here for?"

Like a fool I told him about Jacoby. He knew of him, he drugged before the war. He told me this after I had let out the number of his house in Maida Vale. The moment I was outside I realized my mistake; I should have called on Cameron instead. Passing through the Burlington Arcade, I met Chiffham. He intimated that he wanted a word with me, so we walked up and down in front of the Hotel Bristol. "You're a bold man," he began, "to be seen with Ames just now."

"How's that?"

"He's coming a cropper; we've known it for a long tune.

"Please explain. I haven't the least notion what you mean."

"You must know that his friends are most-ly undesirables."

"Then why do you go to see him."

"I'm all right. Mrs. Harvey Williams sees after that. You see she's writing a book about London types, and I find her copy. Don't you worry about me, I know which side my bread's buttered; but you're such a kid."

"I'm on my own, if that's what you're driving at. But do tell me more about Ames; what has he done?"

"He introduces people and they say he gets money for putting motor-thieves on to stunts. You saw for yourself just now that he procures dope."

"Has he ever been in prison?"

"Not yet; he likes you, doesn't he?"

I held my tongue.

"Well, I don't want to put you against your friend, who is an acquaintance of mine, but I shouldn't run any errands for him, if I were you. I must be getting now. So long."

He turned westwards, and I strolled leisurely to Soho.

XLVIII

I met Dorothy as arranged, and she complained of my listlessness, but did not ask
where I had been, so I could not use the lie
I had ready for her, a most useful one, by the
way, the cinema; you can always say that you
have dropped into one of an afternoon with
perfect naturalness.

"Why are you always dreaming?" she asked
me over the tiny scrap of chicken they gave us.
"Don't you ever want to do anything, to make
your name?"

"If I once did that," I said, "1 should feel a
complete sham."

"Now you're cynical; you mean that all
acknowledged geniuses are shams."

"I never implied such a thing," I returned,
"but that's how it strikes me. You want me to
say to myself, 'I'm Bollond, I'm a great man,
I'm one now, but people don't see it, it's up

to me to make them see it.' Why should I do anything of the kind? If I'm any good, people will find out sometime or other; if I'm not, why should I sweat my life out, trying to impose on them?"

"Nothing is ever done without trying," she said. "Perhaps you've heard of Lomas Bredill."

"The music-hall singer?"

"Yes. Well, that man was made entirely by his wife, and she kept in the background all the time. When they married, he was a green-room habitue and she was playing principal boy at the Islington Pantomime. Nobody knows how they pulled along in the early stages; I think, but am not sure, that she found him a scene-shifter's job. Anyway, they were married, and gradually she got him to see that he had opportunities like other people, if he would only use them. And you see what he is today, much better known than his wife; but he always gives her the credit for his successes.'

"Very nice of her, I'm sure," I said, "and I've no doubt he's happy, more than I should be under the circumstances; everlasting indebtedness is a dreadful complaint to suffer from."

"Oh, you naughty boy, have you been reading Bernard Shaw?"

"Yes, I found all his plays at Jacoby's and skimmed about a third of them. I thank God for Irishmen, don't you?"

"What do you know about Irishmen?"

"More than you think. My mother was an Irishwoman."

"You mean that you have Irish blood, and understand them better than I, who haven't?"

"And what do you know about them?"

"I've slept with—let me see—one, two."

"Were they nice to you?"

"Oh, quite, but they never seemed to want anything."

"Like me."

"Not in the least like you."

"Sorry. Well, what I say is that an Irish person, I include women, of course, does a service without being asked (you can't get them to do anything for the asking), and that is about the biggest service they could do you; quite possibly they do it unconsciously. I haven't a theory about that yet. But that's why I thank God for them."

"Tell me about your mother," she said. "I believe I am beginning to understand you."

But I was not to be drawn on that topic, and this closed our restaurant talk. Afterwards we discussed the books we read in our childhood, and discovered to our surprise that we had practically brought ourselves up on *Jack Sheppard*. It was, we were sure, the most immoral book ever written, and yet was to be had, perhaps not, in stock, of any bookseller. She said she believed if she heard more music she would have been a better character. As it was, when she felt very hostile to the world, hating everyone and wanting to spite them, she walked into the Queen's or Albert Hall. She had been encouraged in this habit by a friend, a young pianist, whose brother constantly got into trouble; he was an incorrigible thief, but she did not mind, though she had a proud spirit, but listened to music and forgot her miseries. We agreed to go to a Sunday concert next day. I slept with her that night, really slept. Had I been alone, I should have lain awake, I had so much to think of.

XLIX

I cannot say at what hour I awoke, but the room was grey. I turned over and looked at Dorothy, and the odd thought struck me that she might be dead, she was lying so very still. I restrained myself from attempting to wake her and went to sleep again. This time I dreamed a dream which I still have cause to remember. I was walking down a London street, when a man, of whom, however, I have no recollection, came up to me and said he would show me round. So I gave myself up to him, and we went about together, meeting the most extraordinary characters, with whom he seemed to be on excellent terms. At first he apologized for not introducing me, but after the sixth person he made a point of doing so. For three or four days after this dream I remembered all the people I met (I have met none of them so far in real life) and could describe them. At the moment I can only see two of them clearly, the rest are smudgy and almost shadows. There was a young man with fair hair, pink complexion, and delightful manners, who said he was making a study of all the birds in London; more than once he had seen a wren in a crowded thoroughfare, flitting between the traffic, and he knew for certain that there was a pair of owls in Lincoln's Inn Fields. Addressing himself to me, he remarked that I should do very well, but I ought to be more certain of myself, if I didn't resent the suggestion; he then spoke to my friend about the difficulty of obtaining taxis. I think his name was Rauder, at least so it sounded. Then there was a girl, Kitty Fisher; she did not wait to be introduced but said, "Oh, it's Mr. Bollond, I knew we should meet; now tell me, is it true that you never use hair oil? I can hardly believe it."

That was all she said to me, which was disappointing, because her manner was so friendly that I thought she would stand talking to me for a long time, or at least listen to what I had to say, and I was most anxious to impress her as a nice person. She had round violet eyes and a cluster of chestnut curls, and wore pearl ear-rings. My friend told her that we would meet that evening at a restaurant.

There was one peculiarity about all these people: they held their heads on one side when they talked.

At last I complained of fatigue, for we must have walked several miles in a more or less circular course, as we repassed the same streets time after time; so we went into a bar and drank cherry brandies. At the third glass I woke up, exclaiming, "Am I really a West End pest?"

"Of course not," said a voice, Dorothy's, adding, "You didn't know that you were talking aloud."

"What else did I say?" I asked.

"That's all," she said.

"But give your reasons for what you said just now."

"You're not the thing you said you were, because you don't live on women; that type usually does."

"It's the women's fault," I said; "they drag men down, because they like men to live on them; it gives them a secure sense of moral superiority. It's always a woman that ruins a man ultimately; another man may have led him astray, put him on the wrong road, but the woman gets him caught out in the long run."

"I quite agree with you," she said with conviction.

I date my friendship with her from that moment; until then neither of us had been sure of the other. Here was a thorough woman who saw things from the male aspect.

Here the MS. breaks off. Reginald Bollond went out for a swim that February evening and never returned alive. Dorothy Earle tried to remonstrate with him as to the madness of going into the sea at that time of year, but he answered that he felt dirty, hadn't had a proper wash since he left London, and wanted to be clean. She saw him leave the house, with a towel over his arm, but did not walk down to the beach with him; he had told her that he won a diving-cup at school. His body was washed ashore the following day, and lies buried in Pevensey churchyard. Those who knew him best say that he was incapable of suicide, and I believe them.

It will be necessary briefly to enumerate the events between the last entry and the writer's death, as far as ascertainable.

After breakfast on the Sunday morning he walked round to Cameron, feeling the want of a man with whom to exchange ideas. Cameron told him that Jacoby was a drug-taker, and would probably fall back on the habit now Bollond had gone. Cameron called at Maida Vale that afternoon, and learned that Jacoby had been found dead in his bed that morning, from an overdose of veronal. Mrs. Jacoby was at first inclined to regard Bollond as the mainspring of the tragedy, but Cameron, who was everyone's good angel at this time, persuaded her to a saner view. Jacoby had made a will ten days previously, in which he left "all I have to leave to Reginald Bollond, the only friend I ever had".

No one suggested that he had made this will under improper suggestion, and Bollond was unaware of its existence. On Tuesday Mrs. Jacoby moved to an hotel. On Friday Roderick Ames was arrested on a charge of procuring cocaine; he said in his statement at the police court that Reginald Bollond was one of the people who wanted it. The police went to Dorothy Earle's lodging and arrested Bollond on suspicion, but he was released, as nothing could be brought against him beyond the bare fact of his acquaintance with Ames. He was, however, subpoenaed as a witness when the case came on at the Central Criminal Court. He spent Christmas in London, not with his aunt. At Hugh Cameron's instance, so I believe, but cannot be sure, Mrs. Jacoby lent her Pevensey cottage to Dorothy and Bollond.

Bollond went down first, and was joined by Dorothy five days later. She describes him as flustered, but not in the least depressed, and greatly relieved by finding that he was able to write an account of himself.

Lucy married Mr. Castle a fortnight after Bollond's funeral, Ames is in prison, Dorothy is travelling abroad with Mrs. Jacoby; Bollond's brothers say Reggie would have refused to touch Jacoby's money.

A PARTIAL LIST OF SNUGGLY BOOKS

G. ALBERT AURIER *Elsewhere and Other Stories*
CHARLES BARBARA *My Lunatic Asylum*
S. HEZOLNRY BERTHOUD *Misanthropic Tales*
LÉON BLOY *The Tarantulas' Parlor and Other Unkind Tales*
ÉLÉMIR BOURGES *The Twilight of the Gods*
CYRIEL BUYSSE *The Aunts*
JAMES CHAMPAGNE *Harlem Smoke*
FÉLICIEN CHAMPSAUR *The Latin Orgy*
BRENDAN CONNELL *Metrophilias*
BRENDAN CONNELL *Spells*
BRENDAN CONNELL (editor)
    The World in Violet: An Anthology of EnglishDecadent Poetry
RAFAELA CONTRERAS *The Turquoise Ring and Other Stories*
DANIEL CORRICK (editor)
    Ghosts and Robbers: An Anthology of German Gothic Fiction
ADOLFO COUVE *When I Think of My Missing Head*
QUENTIN S. CRISP *Aiaigasa*
LUCIE DELARUE-MARDRUS *The Last Siren and Other Stories*
LADY DILKE *The Outcast Spirit and Other Stories*
CATHERINE DOUSTEYSSIER-KHOZE
    The Beauty of the Death Cap
ÉDOUARD DUJARDIN *Hauntings*
BERIT ELLINGSEN *Now We Can See the Moon*
ERCKMANN-CHATRIAN *A Malediction*
ALPHONSE ESQUIROS *The Enchanted Castle*
ENRIQUE GÓMEZ CARRILLO *Sentimental Stories*
DELPHI FABRICE *Flowers of Ether*
DELPHI FABRICE *The Red Sorcerer*
DELPHI FABRICE *The Red Spider*
BENJAMIN GASTINEAU *The Reign of Satan*
EDMOND AND JULES DE GONCOURT *Manette Salomon*
REMY DE GOURMONT *From a Faraway Land*
REMY DE GOURMONT *Morose Vignettes*
GUIDO GOZZANO *Alcina and Other Stories*
GUSTAVE GUICHES *The Modesty of Sodom*
EDWARD HERON-ALLEN *The Complete Shorter Fiction*
EDWARD HERON-ALLEN *Three Ghost-Written Novels*
J.-K. HUYSMANS *The Crowds of Lourdes*
J.-K. HUYSMANS *Knapsacks*
COLIN INSOLE *Valerie and Other Stories*
JUSTIN ISIS *Pleasant Tales II*